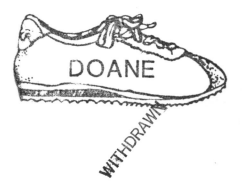

DOANE

WITHDRAWN

I Wear the
Morning Star

Also by Jamake Highwater

FICTION
The Sun, He Dies
Anpao
The Ceremony of Innocence
Journey to the Sky
Legend Days
Eyes of Darkness

POETRY
Moonsong Lullaby

NONFICTION
Many Smokes, Many Moons: *A Chronology of
American Indian History Through Indian Art*

Dance: *Rituals of Experience*

Ritual of the Wind: *North American Indian
Ceremonies, Music and Dance*

Song from the Earth: *North American Indian Painting*

The Sweet Grass Lives On: *Fifty Contemporary
North American Indian Artists*

The Primal Mind: *Vision and Reality in Indian America*

Arts of the Indian Americas: *Leaves from the Sacred Tree*

Words in the Blood: *An Anthology of Contemporary
Native American Literature* (editor)

Jamake Highwater

I Wear the Morning Star

PART THREE OF

The Ghost Horse Cycle

Harper & Row, Publishers

NEW YORK

Library of Congress Cataloging in Publication Data
Highwater, Jamake.
  I wear the morning star.

  (Pt. three of the Ghost Horse cycle)
  "A Charlotte Zolotow book."
  Summary: Amana's grandson Sitko, growing up in a
hostile white world that tries to make him renounce his
heritage as an American Indian, struggles to fulfill
his talents as an artist.
  1. Indians of North America—Juvenile fiction.
[1. Indians of North America—Fiction.   2. Artists—
Fiction]   I. Title.   II. Series: Highwater, Jamake.
Ghost Horse cycle ; pt. 3.
PZ7.H5443Iw 1986   [Fic]   85-45258
ISBN 0-06-022355-3
ISBN 0-06-022356-1 (lib. bdg.)

In memory of

ALTA BLACK
(1888–1978)

Who told the duckling about the swan

We cannot express the light in nature
because we have not the sun.
We can only express the light
we have in ourselves.

Arthur Dove

I Wear the
Morning Star

One

My mother led me away.
It was in the evening, when the birds were still singing, that she led me away from the house of Grandma Amana.

My grandmother knelt in front of me and embraced me with such intensity that my shoulders hurt. Then she covered her face and turned away as my mother pulled me along after her, out into an evening so vast and empty that I began to cry. I was too young to understand what was happening to me, but the groans of my grandmother and the expression on my mother's face made me feel that something terrible was taking place. A great stone began to burn in my belly. I could no longer hear the song of the birds, but only a fierce and wild cry that was tumbling from my own mouth.

"Stop it!" my mother shouted as her hand lashed my cheek. "My God, child, please stop crying!" she exclaimed as she dragged me from Grandma Amana's house.

That is when the silence overtook me, suddenly and

completely, as if something wide and free within me closed itself away from the world forever. The sobs died in my throat, and nothing remained but the great burning stone in my belly. It was on that day when the birds were singing that I stumbled silently into the strange new life that awaited me.

It was Saturday. It was a muddy Saturday. I stood dumbfounded, staring at the children who raced up and down the hallway, while my mother talked quietly to the lady seated at the desk, answering her questions self-consciously.

"Sitko," my mother said. "His name is Sitko Ghost Horse. He has one older brother named Reno . . . yes, that's right, Reno. No, he's not at home. . . . Reno has been at another boarding school for about a year."

The lady wrote everything down on a long yellow paper. The rapidly moving pen and the long line of words it produced seemed to worry my mother. She tilted her head to the side in an effort to read what the lady was writing about her. She tried to explain: "I really wanted to keep Sitko at home, but his father . . ."

"What about his father?" the woman interrupted. "Where's he from? What's his background?"

"Cherokee . . . I think his father is Cherokee."

The woman looked up with an expression of impatience. "You think?" she asked.

"He's Cherokee," my mother repeated nervously, squeezing my hand. "He's definitely Cherokee. And, well, he went off . . . about four months ago. And we haven't heard from him, and we just can't manage. Not without Jamie. That's my husband, Jamie Ghost Horse. . . ."

"And you . . . are you also Indian?"

"Why no," my mother lied, sounding as if she were astonished by the question. "I'm French. I'm French-Canadian. My maiden name was Bonneville. Jemina Bonneville."

It was a rainy Saturday. The vast and empty sky was filled with gray rain, and in my belly was a stone. That's all I can remember. The terrible burning in my stomach. The rain. And the forlorn eyes of all those children who collected in the doorway and peered at us, until the woman at the desk sent them away.

Everything I had ever feared was happening. To be lost in the darkness. To be alone in a place without windows. I grasped my mother's hand fiercely, sensing that at any moment she was going to leave. I tried to think of how brave my father would have been. I tried to believe that my mother would not go. But the stone turned slowly in my belly, and it burned.

Then my mother got up quickly, and without looking back at me, she fled from the room.

I shouted but I could not hear my voice. Then I wheeled around as the woman caught me in her firm grasp. She was smiling at me, but her fingers hurt my arms. "I bet your name is Sitko," she was saying. "Is that what your name is?"

I couldn't free myself from her grip, and so I stared into her pale face and tried desperately not to cry.

"Don't you want to tell me your name? It's such a nice name . . . so unusual," she said in a tone so artificial it frightened me.

I leaned away from her, afraid I was going to be sick.

"Such a big boy. . . . You're not going to cry, now, are you," she said as she pulled me down the immense hallways where the children stopped and stared and whispered. I searched the doorways for my mother, but she was gone. I clenched my teeth each time I felt tears coming into my eyes. But I could not stop the burning stone that was slowly rising into my chest. I could not stop the fear that thickened in my throat. And then I began to groan, for I realized I was urinating in my pants.

"Shame on you!" the woman snapped, pushing me backward into a dark room and slamming the door. "You just stay in there, young man, until you learn to behave!"

I banged on the door. I shouted and begged to be let out. And then I fell silent as I heard her footsteps moving away.

Now I was in the dark. It was a rainy Saturday, and I was shut up in a dark and windowless room. My mother was surely gone for good. And my beloved Grandma Amana was far away . . . from this terrible place where people left their children when they didn't want them anymore.

I searched the dark room, seeing the faint white glimmer of owls. I whimpered and backed against the wall. I did not move. I waited . . . I don't know for how long I waited for the monsters of the room to attack me. Then suddenly a brilliant light burned into my sleep, and I awakened with the terrible realization that all that I had known and all that I had loved was gone. I had entered the dark room I always feared, and it was here in the darkness that I would have to live the rest of my life.

The Home was called Star of Good Hope. Once or twice a week a mother came down the long hallway, pulling along a boy or a girl. No matter where you were at Star of Good Hope you could always hear the weeping of the new children. And when you peeked into the office, you could see on the mothers' faces the tormented expression that I had seen on my own mother's face. Then, before dark, the mothers would leave. And most of them never came back again. Now the long hallways were empty. The children searched all the rooms of Star of Good Hope for their parents. They called out in their sleep. But there were no mothers or fathers at the Home. There was just the housemother and the schoolmaster and the men and women in uniforms. People without children of their own.

Sometimes, on Sundays, a man or a woman sat in the housemother's parlor, waiting to see one of the children. Nobody came to see me. At first I sat on the curb in front of the white building where I lived, watching for Grandma Amana, but she did not come. When it began to get dark and the other children returned from outings with their parents, I knew I wasn't one of the lucky ones—the ones who still had mothers and fathers. I knew I had been abandoned. So I wanted to die. I wanted to go to sleep until my life was over, until years and years of Sundays passed and all the parents had gone home, and the sky had turned dark forever. I wanted to sleep until I was no longer a child and could pack my things and leave Star of Good Hope, walking past the headmaster's house, down the lane that circled the little pine forest, past the church where we sang on Sunday mornings, and past the fountain with its statue of a boy and girl standing beneath a bright green umbrella. I wanted to walk down the road that stretched beyond the painted line the children were not allowed to cross, through the gate at the road's end, where the railroad tracks ran into a long and distant silence.

I walked across the dormitory in my muslin under-wear and opened my locker. Everything they gave me to wear was baggy and smelled of mothballs and strong soap. I studied myself in the mirror for a long time, amazed by my ugliness. Somehow—in just a matter of weeks—I had become deformed. My arms and legs were too long. I was so skinny that I nearly disappeared from the mirror when I turned sideways. Something terrible had started happening to my body. And though nobody had noticed it, I realized that I was going to be a freak.

In only a month I had grown taller. My cuffs were up to my ankles. In another year I would be seven or eight feet tall! I would have to stay in bed and pretend to be sick so nobody would notice that I was becoming a freak.

9 / I Wear the Morning Star

"The poor child . . ." they would whisper, *"he's deformed. Just take a look at him."*

As I turned away from the mirror I was filled with a terrible realization: I could never be like other children. It was a revelation that tumbled down upon me from the mirror. A terrible thought overtook me. I would spend my life in an outer circle, removed from other people.

"The poor child . . . he doesn't know who he is. Just take a look at him."

The voices rattled the mirror. I backed away in fear, sensing the darkness within that silver glass. Its prophecy haunted me as I pushed my feet into tennis shoes and pulled on the brown sweater that was covered with foxtails, wedged like tiny arrows into the wool. I imagined I was a martyr. I imagined I was Gunga Din . . . until the mirror mocked me with my reflection. *God, what a mess you are!* How could anybody be so ugly? No matter what I did, no matter how long I spent trying to look like other children, the glass laughed at me. In the morning, I would hurry into the lavatory to see if the mirror had changed its mind. But my reflection didn't change. I was too brown. My hair was too coarse. I was too tall and too skinny, and my nose and chin and even my lips were too big. *"Nigger lips, nigger lips, nigger lips . . ."* the mirror whispered. *"Nigger lips,"* the children called after me.

It was on one long-ago morning at Star of Good Hope that I came to understand who I am.

It was Sunday. The other children had gone to the village, but I wouldn't go with them. They were not my friends. There was no one left on the little street of the Home. And, as I wandered among the trees that lined the pavement, I could hear the whispers of the house-mothers who watched from behind the blank, dark windows of the houses. I hurried away from their voices, which gradually faded into the babble of the fountain's water, which trickled over the green umbrella and fell silvery and blue into the pool. The water moved so slowly that it had grown long, mossy beards upon the chins of the boy and girl who hovered under the umbrella. I sat on the curb and imagined that I was a statue, safe and snug forever beneath a green umbrella. With pink cheeks and red lips and lovely soft blond hair. The driplets of water sang to me, ringing outward in a chorus of sighs. A few leaves drifted down. A large yellow cat came to drink at the fountain, turning, as it swallowed, first into a leopard and then into a tiger. Its passionate roar sent all the housemothers fleeing from their windows. I laughed with delight. But my voice startled the tiger, and it vanished without a trace.

It was on that Sunday of the yellow cat that I looked up and saw a familiar figure coming cautiously toward me. It was an older boy . . . a handsome fellow with pale blue eyes and a look of pride that he wore like a buffalo robe. He was gazing at me as he approached, as though he was trying to understand my peculiar face, trying to figure out why I was sitting alone by the fountain. I became apprehensive because I knew he would realize, as he drew nearer, that I was a deformity. Of all the people at Star of Good Hope whom I had met since my mother had abandoned me, only this young man seemed to look at me. I hoped he might be a friend, for I had no friends. And that hope made me more apprehensive as he came closer and stared down at me.

"What's your name?" he asked in a familiar voice, sitting on the curb beside me and lightly touching my long hair as if it amazed him.

I was too shy to respond. I looked away, for the familiar ring of his voice touched me so deeply that it brought tears to my eyes.

"Do you live here?" he asked. "Or are you lost?"

"I live here, and I am lost," I said.

Then the young man laughed joyously and embraced me. "Sitko! Sitko! It's me . . . It's Reno, your brother."

"No . . . no . . ." I mumbled, weeping openly at the cruel joke of this young man. "My brother is gone. They took him away. He is gone."

"Look at this signet ring that was our father's!" the young man exclaimed. "Then tell me if I am lying!"

I do not recall what happened next. The memory has turned into many colors heaped one upon the other. A deluge of yellow for our smiles, and green for the umbrella that shaded our reunion, and blue for the love I saw in my brother's eyes.

It was on that Sunday of blue eyes and yellow tigers that Reno came out of the shadows of the past to live at Star of Good Hope.

Two

I was proud when Reno moved into the dormitory. How beautiful he was! How everyone admired him!

When he walked among the children of Star of Good Hope, everyone smiled at him. His shirt was starched and his tennis shoes gleamed. No one in the world had such clean shoes. I watched him every night while he scrubbed his tennis shoes. He even bleached the laces, filling the lavatory with a stench so strong that it made me delirious.

He was sixteen, and already he shaved. All his pimples had disappeared and his voice was handsome and low. When he sang and played his guitar his voice was beautiful. And it didn't bother him when the children came into the room to listen to him. Nothing frightened Reno. He grew stronger and taller when people looked at him. His eyes glowed with power and he opened up like a Chinese fan, with ever-widening beauty. *He was a butterfly.*

I was fascinated and frightened by his perfection. I loved to look at him. I would stand at the window and watch him race around the baseball field while the other boys cheered. I admired Reno so much that I dissolved into a dream where he was stretched above the world like an eternal blue sky. I became silent, unable to speak to him unless he first spoke to me. I loved and dreaded his attention. I was tormented when he said, "This is my brother." For I could see the indifference of the children as they glanced at me. Standing next to Reno I felt small and worthless. I tried not to call attention to myself. I did not speak. I withdrew into the shadows where I could watch him without being noticed. And within my seclusion—like a cocoon—I began to be transformed, limb by limb, cell by cell, until I no longer existed. Reno was the butterfly, but I was a shadow, and I could go wherever I wished to go on his marvelous, wide wings.

One day the housemother told me that it was my birthday.

"Do you know what that means?" she asked, reaching toward me with a contrite look in her eyes.

I winced at her fingers, for I could not bear to be touched.

"There is someone to see you," she said impatiently.

I trembled at the thought of having to face a stranger. Backing away, I ran in search of Reno and found him in the dormitory.

"Quick!" he exclaimed. "Get under the bed and don't say a word or I'll never speak to you again! D'you hear what I said?"

I scrambled under my bed and tried not to breathe, in fear that Reno would hate me. Then I heard someone come into the room, and I peeked out to see who it was. A tall, dark man was standing in the doorway.

"Where's your brother?" the man asked.

"He's not here! He's not here! Why don't you stay away! We don't want to see you!" Reno shouted as he turned and ran from the room.

The man stood there silently.

After a long time, I could see the man leave, and I crept from under the bed.

Reno was hiding in the toilet, sitting and sulking, his head propped up on his hands. I gazed at him in silence, afraid of his anger and not knowing what to say.

"You didn't talk to him, did you?" he muttered without looking at me.

I shook my head earnestly.

"He's no good," Reno said solemnly, an uncommon sorrow filling his eyes. "He's just a drunkard and a bastard, and he's no good."

I nodded in agreement, but I did not understand. Reno shrugged when he saw my bewilderment.

"He used to be our father," he said in a whisper. "He used to live with us. But he's no good," Reno muttered sadly. "I don't know why he comes around here 'cause he never cared about us when he was our father."

I turned slowly, filled with remorse and dismay, urgently trying to summon back the face of the tall, dark man who used to be my father. I wanted to save some small recollection of him, for I had no other memories. I could not recall where or when I was born or the places I had lived or the people I had known. I could only remember the face of Grandma Amana on the day my mother took me away from her. Nothing else remained. My father had no face or name. He had left no trace upon my mind. And so I struggled against the immense soft gray wall of memory, trying to bring him back. But I could only recall the long, low sound of his retreating footsteps.

That night it rained. Reno did not come down to dinner, and I sat, unable to eat or speak, under the disapproving gaze of the housemother.

"You will not leave this table, young man, until you've cleaned your plate," she said, noisily pushing back her chair and ushering the children out of the dining room.

Then the light went out.

I sat in the dim light streaming in from the pantry. I felt ill as I looked down at the cold stew in my dish. I wanted to shout after the housemother. I wanted to tell her that I would starve myself to death before I would eat such garbage!

The good things Grandma Amana used to make for me had kept me strong, but the food at Star of Good Hope was making me into a deformity. I was getting skinnier and skinnier each day. And I was helpless. So I sat in the darkness, feeling ill.

Grandma Amana! Help me to eat this terrible food!

But I could not swallow. The colder the stew got the more greasy and dreadful it tasted.

Then I heard a sound. I peered behind me, fearful that the headmaster had come to give me a thrashing. To my relief I saw Reno creeping into the dining room. He gestured for me to be silent. He stood in the doorway for a long time before he cautiously came to my side. I was afraid he would scold me for embarrassing him, for getting into trouble by refusing to eat. I trembled as Reno stood over me in the dimness, saying nothing. Then he carefully unlocked the window beside the table. Silently he pushed it wide open. A rainy breeze swept down upon me. He quickly took the dish from in front of me, and when he returned it to the table it was empty. Then, without a word, he hurried away.

I tried not to weep as I lowered my head to the table, overcome by the realization that my brother truly loved me. And in the dark dining room of Star of Good Hope I resolved that I would try, harder than I had ever tried, to please Reno and to make him proud of me.

"If you really want to show me that you love me," Reno told me, "stop talking about Grandma Amana, and stop using those crazy words she taught you, for Christ's sake."

"But Reno . . ."

"And that's another thing . . . don't interrupt when I'm talking to you, Sitko. Just listen to what I'm telling you, 'cause it's for your own good."

I nodded silently.

"So, y'hear, just forget all that stuff and try to fit in. Things are bad enough without letting everybody know what kind of a family we come from."

"But, Reno," I whispered very quietly so nobody would hear me, "we can't help it if our father's a drunkard. We can't help it if we're . . . Indians."

"I'm no damn Indian! D'you understand what I'm saying to you, Sitko? I don't want you to say stuff like that or I swear I'll hit you!"

I winced and shook my head as a feeling of panic filled me.

Reno sighed regretfully and put his hand gently upon my shoulder. "Okay, okay, you know damn well I wouldn't hit you. But you just listen good to what I'm telling you, Sitko. I'm old enough to know about things like this. Nobody's got to be an Indian if he doesn't want to be. And that's a fact. That's exactly what Mom told me. Nobody has to be anything like that if he doesn't want to be. Do you hear me?"

I nodded anxiously.

"Are you listening to me, Sitko?"

I swallowed hard and nodded once again, hoping he would believe me.

"Okay, then, you just tell me exactly what I said," Reno insisted.

Despite my desire to please my brother, I could not stop thinking about Grandma Amana. I felt I was betraying her by saying I was not Indian.

But Reno kept looking hard at me, until I finally stammered, "I won't do it anymore, Reno. I swear that

I won't say anything ever again about . . . about it."

He grinned at me with approval.

"You be a good boy," he said, "and next Saturday I'll talk the housemother into letting us go to the movies together!"

His expression brightened, and he hugged me and rocked me in his arms. It felt marvelous to be held and loved by him. But even as I enjoyed Reno's affection, still I felt troubled and guilty. I could not stop thinking of Grandma Amana. I could not rid myself of the terrible feeling that I had betrayed her.

Reno kept his promise, and on the last Saturday of the month, the luckiest of us were lined up in front of the fountain by the housemother. Then, after being carefully counted and lectured about staying in line and behaving properly, we were marched off to the movie matinee.

It was in the darkness of that little motion-picture theater that I came to understand why Reno did not want to be an Indian anymore. I sat expectantly as the shadows darted across the screen. The brave soldiers of the fort were being attacked by dark, savage men with feathers in their hair . . . cruel animals sneaking through the tall grass with knives between their teeth, shooting flaming arrows into the house of a pretty blond lady. She screamed again and again and fell to her knees before her husband, crying: "Kill me! Don't let them take me alive! Please promise that you will kill me!"

I came out into the evening, shaken and bewildered.

Reno gave me a dark look and touched my shoulder with compassion as we silently joined the march back to Star of Good Hope. I could not speak of it, but I was horrified by the brutality of the film. That night my sleep was filled with nightmares. And in the morning, when I brushed my teeth, I saw in the mirror the face that had terrified me in my dreams.

The next day, Reno sat silently in the barbershop and watched intently as the short man with the bald head drew my long hair into his clumsy hands and cut it off, lock by lock, letting the strands of thick, black hair fall to the floor in a heap. Reno raised no objection, and I knew he was glad to see my long hair cut, but I could tell from his expression that he loathed the housemother who had ordered the haircut as a punishment because I would not eat the wretched food of Star of Good Hope. I hated the little barber who seemed to take particular pleasure in hacking off my hair. It was the only thing about me that I liked.

"Now this will make a real man of you!" he exclaimed as he snipped handfuls of hair.

My shame was so great, I closed my eyes. Grandmother Amana had told us about the power that exists in our hair. And she had braided my hair every morning and refused to let anyone near me when Jemina and Reno had wanted my hair to be cut so I wouldn't look like some kind of strange and crazy child. But Grandma Amana shook her head: "*Sa!* . . . No!" she would mutter in a voice so low that it frightened everyone. "*Sa! Ko-*

da-yo-toks-pas, sa! No! Do you hear me, no!"

Now my grandmother was far away and could not protect me. I sat forlornly under the large white sheet that completely covered me. I sat silently and stared at Reno, while the locks fell and my ancient power died on the floor. Then, to my amazement, tears filled Reno's eyes and he hurried from the barber's shop.

Three

————————————

S ummer. And at last I could escape the confinement
of the dormitory where there was no place for me
to avoid the peevishness of the children. I did not have
to play their fool. Now the world was turning yellow as
sunlight pierced the sky. The mood of the children
changed abruptly. They broke out into the freedom of
the sunny, green world, hurrying off in little groups,
each with its own leader, followers and fools. I was free
of them. Now there was room enough for me to hide
in a corner of the playground, where I could watch Reno
hit the ball and make it sail like a white bird far over
the heads of the cheering boys.

He was more perfect than ever. He strutted around
with his brilliant tan, glowing golden and looking like a
Spanish gypsy. Once, as he pranced effortlessly around
the bases, he veered toward me, coming almost to my
side, and he winked as he passed, so that my heart leaped
with pride.

At night Reno would take me to the library, where

we hid behind the couch, and he read to me. After reading a few stories, he insisted that I watch carefully as he moved his finger along the mysterious marks that became words in his mouth. Now and again he would pause and prompt me to continue, but I did not understand how to make the marks on the page into words. He scolded me when my attention faltered, and my gaze moved from the page to his face. But I preferred to watch his lips as the words miraculously formed upon them and brought the story to life. I could not understand how even someone as smart as Reno could do something so remarkable: how he could turn the marks upon the pages into such marvelous stories that came alive!

I loved the tales Reno read to me, but I did not recall the words. I was afraid that the tales would die if I did not remember them, and so I kept the stories alive inside of me with a succession of bright images which flickered through my mind. I could summon these pictures at will, and when I was alone I surrounded myself with them, basking in the brilliant colors and fantastic figures. These were my words and my stories . . . these images from the stories Reno read to me. I began to cover sheets of paper with them. I had discovered how to bring the images hidden in me to life on paper.

The pictures were my secrets. I hid them under my bed and did not let anyone see them, until one day Reno crept up behind me and looked over my shoulder.

"What are you doing?" he asked. "How did you learn to do that?"

I quickly put my hands over the picture, fearful that Reno would disapprove. But instead of disapproving, he smiled and gently drew my hands away as he gazed at the images.

He touched my shoulder and nodded without speaking. Then he turned and went away.

The next morning when I reached under my bed for my pencil and pictures, I found a large box of crayons and a pad of real drawing paper Reno had left for me! As I sat on the floor and looked at the wonderful colors, a remarkable thought took shape in my mind. Reno liked my pictures! He actually liked something that I had done! It was the first time I had ever won his admiration.

Now each evening, after Reno read to me, I would unroll my secret pictures and show them to him. He never spoke as he gazed at the images from the tales he had read to me the previous evening, but I knew that he was pleased, for a wisp of a smile crossed his serious face and his eyes brightened.

"What is this?" he asked as he lifted a sheet into the light and studied it. "What story is this?"

I was reluctant to answer because the picture was not about a story.

"It's okay, Sitko, you can tell me. What is this supposed to be?"

It was something almost lost, something I vaguely remembered.

"Tell me, what is it, Sitko? Is it a story of your own?"

It was a picture of a tall, dark man standing in a doorway. It was our father.

I was afraid that Reno would be mad, because I knew he didn't want me to have anything to do with the man who used to be our father. But it was pointless to lie.

When I told him the truth, however, he did not get angry. He sat back sadly and fell silent as he continued to gaze at the picture. Then at last he said in a gentle voice, "I remember when I was maybe seven years old. Our father and I helped build a little monument on the side of the highway. It was a monument for soldiers who had died in some past war. I don't know which war it was, but it was the one that happened a long time ago when our father was young. He used to get together with a bunch of Indians and on Sundays they'd dig a lot of holes and pour cement and work on this little monument by the side of the road. I don't know where it was. But I bet it's still standing somewhere out by the highway, half covered with weeds."

Reno reached hesitantly toward my picture, touching it with the tips of his fingers, and then drew them to his lips. "Everything else from those days is gone," he said dolefully. Then he shrugged and laughed dryly. "Jamie was always puffed up about being an Indian. But he didn't know the first thing about it. Grandma Amana spoke the language and grew up with it, but Jamie— well, he was just proud of being Indian 'cause he didn't have anything else to be proud about. He's what they call a *renegade.* All he knew for sure was that he could drink a pint of booze faster than you could pour it. And when he wasn't drunk he was running off with the rodeo. Jamie called himself by all kinds of names in those days.

That's why none of us know who the hell we really are. He dragged me and Mom around with him in his truck. He worked in circuses and rodeos and anything else that would keep him in booze. Sometimes he came home with us. But most of the time he stayed away. I don't know how Ma put up with it for as long as she did. She was maybe sixteen when they got married. She thought he was some big hero. Then she found out he was just a renegade and a drunk. When we moved to the San Fernando Valley, he got work doing stunts . . . falling down and leaping off cliffs for the movies. But that didn't last long. Finally he just walked out on us. And now he wants us to act like he's our father!" Reno said bitterly as he slowly wadded up my picture in his fist and held it to his chest with both hands.

"So now you know about our father," he murmured without looking at me.

Every week Reno counted out the coins he received for chores he did for the man named Bill who ran the laundry at Star of Good Hope. Then Bill would go off to the village where he bought a big bottle of soda pop and a pint of vanilla ice cream for us.

"You two better button up about this or I'll lose my job for sure," he warned, passing Reno the brown bag.

"We won't say a word," Reno promised solemnly.

"Well, have a good time, and don't ruin your dinner," the man said with a smile.

Reno and I went by ourselves to the fragrant eucalyptus trees behind the laundry, sprawling on the cool ground that was piled high with leaves. There Reno carefully mixed the melted ice cream and Seven-Up in glasses that I had spirited away from the dining room one night while I sat over my dinner waiting for Reno to sneak up next to me and throw it out the window.

The ice-cream sodas were delicious. Nothing in the world tasted better than those frothy, cold contraband treats behind the laundry house, under the wind-filled eucalyptus trees. We whispered and laughed together in the lovely summer's day, closer to one another than we had ever been in our lives. I was no longer lonely. I felt safe and at peace for the first time since I had been taken from Grandma Amana. I could even bear the indifference of the other children so long as I knew Reno liked me. I cherished his approval. I grew strong from his smiles and laughter. On those long-ago summer days I came to love my brother so desperately that my heart ached at the sight of him.

Summer ended, and torrents of leaves began to fall, tumbling along the windy streets where the children trampled upon them as they dashed out of the one-room schoolhouse where classes had begun again.

"One, two, three . . ." I tried valiantly to learn, but I was hopelessly behind the other children my age. The teacher, who had to instruct a large class consisting of all nine grades, had no patience with me. I dreaded being called upon to recite in class. Even when I knew the answers to my teacher's questions, I could not bring myself to speak amid the giggles and whispers of the other students, who seemed to take particular delight in my awkwardness.

"I asked you a question, Sitko," she said as I stared at her in silence.

"Sitko!" the teacher repeated sternly, "I asked you something, young man! For goodness' sake, child, stop chewing on that pencil and speak up!"

I was so embarrassed that I could not speak.

"You do understand English," she exclaimed to the delight of the students. "I asked you the name of the largest river in the United States. It has an Indian name, Sitko, so you should know something about it!"

I quickly glanced at Reno who was slouching miserably in his seat with his face turned away. I did not know what to do or say, and I became so confused and frightened that I whispered, "I do not know. . . ."

"What did you say? Speak up, child, so we can hear what you are saying."

I began to tremble. And before I knew what I was doing I had leaped to my feet and shouted again and again, "*Ne-mots-che-ne-pa!* . . . I don't know!"

My answer caused shrieks of laughter. The teacher ordered me out of the room.

I could not look at Reno as I passed his seat, for I knew that I had broken my solemn promise not to say the words that Grandma Amana had taught me.

That night Reno did not come into the dining room when I sat silently over my cold dish in the dark. And on Saturday he did not take me to the movies. He did not come to the eucalyptus grove behind the laundry. So I knew he hated me.

It started to rain and the earth became laden with mud and rotting leaves. I put my jacket over my head and ran as fast as I could in large circles in the driving rain. I ran and ran until I fell into the mud with exhaustion.

That night I sat in a corner and watched my brother hold hands with a girl named Wilma who had a very large chest. I had never seen anybody with such a fat chest. I stared at her and hated her for taking Reno away from me. I couldn't understand why he would want to have anything to do with a girl. But the older boys liked to talk about Wilma when the housemother wasn't listening. And as the weeks went by, they envied Reno because he told them that Wilma sometimes let him feel her chest when they hid behind the gymnasium.

"Boy, isn't that something!" the boys exclaimed. "Reno sure gets all the breaks!"

But I thought Wilma was more of a deformity than I was.

Now I rarely saw my brother. He no longer embraced me. He didn't wink at me when he hit a home run, he didn't care when the other children tormented me. He was with Wilma almost all the time. And gradually I began to drift off by myself.

I had no friends. I did not know how to talk to people. And if they tried to be friendly, I was so embarrassed that I fled. I lived within my cocoon where I could be a beautiful butterfly like Reno. I spent the days making pictures filled with all the lovely colors and images that lived inside of me. But when people looked at me they could not see the place where my beauty lived. In their eyes I could see my ugliness reflected back at me. To them I was never a butterfly. I was a skinny little boy, with funny hair and a big nose.

When games were played I never got my turn. I could not understand why people hated me before they knew anything about me. I sometimes tried to make the other children notice me, but they responded as if I didn't exist. They seemed full of camaraderie and high spirits as they rushed into the playground, but I was always left behind. Slowly as the days went by and Reno became more and more remote, I decided that I could not blame them for ignoring somebody who was a deformity. I turned away from the playground, taking refuge behind the couch in the library where I spent hours filling pages with the beauty lost within me that no one else could see. I didn't know where such images came from, but foxes and owls and strange, unknown lands appeared in the pictures I drew—rising in smoke from the dark place in my heart where Grandma Amana's songs glowed luminous and blue.

When winter was ending and the birds came back into the budding trees, I emerged from behind the couch and went in search of springtime, for there were no crayons or sheets of paper left, and without them I was desolate.

I silently watched the children as they were liberated from winter's confinement and raced headlong into the playground which, for me, was a forbidden land. I thought I was the only one hated because there was something wrong with me. But that spring, I noticed two other children who were always excluded and left behind. At first I had detested them just as everybody else did, but slowly I realized we had a common bond. And once I acknowledged this, I reluctantly became one of them. That decision of my childhood was bitter, for once I accepted that I was an outsider I could never be anything but an outsider.

What drew us together and what made us outsiders was our ugliness.

Freddy had carrot-red hair and acted like a girl. Suzie was fat and wore thick glasses that made her eyes look huge. And I was a ridiculously skinny giant, towering unnaturally over the other leftover people as we marched together around Star of Good Hope. I was surely the most deformed of the trio.

Every day we found ourselves alone . . . a little gaggle of outsiders. We could not escape one another and so we gradually became friends—not because we liked each other, but because we didn't have anybody else. Trapped in our ugliness, we had become friends of necessity.

The three of us created our own games and our own rules. We created charades, collecting bits and pieces for props and costumes. The playground belonged to the other children, but the imagination was the place where we lived! And when our plays were over and I took off my robe and jewels and allowed Freddy to carry them away to their hiding place, I would sit under the eucalyptus trees and plan a marvelous garden—a Chinese garden that we three would plant during the warm spring days.

I knew nothing about a Chinese garden, but the words delighted me, and in my mind I could see a garden like nothing I had ever seen before . . . some place marvelous and strange.

"I'll tell you something secret," I whispered to Freddy and Sue, "if you swear on your lives that you won't tell anybody!"

Their expressions changed as they drew close to me, horses leaping in their eyes.

"Tell us!" Sue begged.

"Well," I whispered, "I am an Indian . . . and that means I know how to make a magic garden!"

Both of my friends nodded with excitement and started prancing happily, until I silenced them with a gesture I had learned from Grandma Amana. "A garden . . ." I whispered mysteriously, overcome by a flood of longing for the green earth. *"A magic garden!"*

Freddy and Sue believed everything I told them that afternoon, but gradually I realized that they were only pretending. They could not understand what was deep within me unless they made it into a game of make-believe. And when the game was over, so were all the miraculous things that happened to us. For me, however, the adventure continued because it was alive inside of me.

I even told Freddy and Sue about the time the Fox had visited me. Their eyes flashed with images of the bright-red animal, rising upon his back legs and dancing around and around as the wind blew into our memories and released the ancient shadows of forgotten ancestors. But they didn't know how to see the Fox, and they didn't know that foxes could speak to people. They only pretended to believe, and maybe that is why they were leftover people.

But I was different. I had one thing none of them had. Grandma Amana had put something into my heart. Within me, very deep inside of me, I possessed a world they couldn't see, a place where the light was blue. And nothing could ever put out the blue flame Grandma Amana had lighted within me. Not Freddy or Sue, and not Reno or the housemother or the teacher. Not even the headmaster of Star of Good Hope!

From Grandma Amana I had learned how to dream myself into existence. From her I had learned that *every-thing* is real.

Teach me to make the earth green!
Amid the earth's panting
amid rising smoke,
I see Grandmother's footprints.
Amid things visible,
I see blades of grass.
Teach me to make the earth green!
May Grandmother's footsteps
fill with grass
and may the animals thrive!

This is the song I sang as I sat beneath the eucalyptus trees at Star of Good Hope and dreamed a garden out of the hard earth. I sang and chanted and danced while Freddy and Sue looked on in amazement. They tried to join me, but they could not say the words, and they could not dance.

Even after many songs and dances the ground beneath the eucalyptus trees was hard and dry. The three of us worked with our hands, hacking and digging with butter knives we stole from the dining room. The little irrigation ditch we dug traveled through the stubborn, brittle clay, from the water faucet up by the laundry down to the grove of eucalyptus trees. It took many days to dig the trench, and then, in May, after several chants and dances, eighteen sweet pea seeds were lovingly buried in the gray, lifeless soil.

I closed my eyes and dreamed hard of many beautiful seedlings awakening within the earth. Every day the water was cautiously turned on after Freddy checked to make sure the housemothers weren't looking, and inch by inch the gray earth turned black with moisture, until at last the little garden drank heavily and fell asleep.

Every morning for three months we assembled at the garden, but there was no sign of life. The earth remained stark and barren.

"You said you knew magic," Freddy said one day. "And we did all the work 'cause you said you're an Indian. But nothing has happened, and you're not Indian! You're just a fake and a liar!"

"Be patient," I said. "The sweet peas will grow! The dances and chants will make them grow!"

Suzie refused to turn on the faucet. "I played your game," she said, "but I won't anymore!"

"Besides," Freddy added, "everybody knows Indians don't go around planting sweet peas! They ride horses! That's what Indians do! And you know as much about horses as you do about sweet peas!"

I tried to explain that things would not grow if you did not believe in them, but Freddy wouldn't listen to me.

"I'm quitting," he said, tossing down his butter knife. "Come on, Sue, let's get out of here."

I stood over the little garden and wept. In the distance I could hear the children cheering Reno as he hit a home run. I could hear Freddy jeering at me as he pulled Sue after him up the hill toward the laundry. Then there was silence.

I lingered at the garden until the light failed in the trees and the dinner bell clanged. I gazed all around me, but I could see nothing but the barren earth. Even Grandma Amana had vanished from my mind.

Now I was alone.

The next time I saw Freddy and Suzie they started patting their mouths with their palms, mocking the songs I had sung.

"Stop that! Stop that!" I shouted.

But they continued until a crowd of children came running toward us and joined the mockery. I stood help-

lessly as they pranced around me, sending up a whirlwind of dust on the vast playground. As the children
laughed, I turned and strode away, my tears blinding
me.

That evening I visited the garden and looked at it in
the long, lingering sunlight that shimmered through the
leaves. Someone had pulled up all the trellises. Someone
had thrown leaves over the ground and trampled it. And
now nothing was left of the Chinese garden.

"I will remember this," I shouted. "I'll remember
what you have done to me today!"

I do not know how long I shouted, but gradually my
outcry was lost in the treetops, and it was dark, and my
dream of sweet peas turned to ashes.

Four

████ ████ ████ ████ ████

The tarantulas of summer had burrowed into the earth, and the winter rain was coming down hard. Under the rain-pelted roof I hid behind the couch while the housemother searched for me.

I lived in my pictures. Since I had run out of paper, I began to use the ends of boxes and anything else I could find in the trash. The only thing that was important to me was my drawing, and I contrived to spend every day in the world of my pictures. There I felt safe. But even behind the couch I could not be alone. A few of the youngest children had discovered my hiding place. They hovered behind me as I worked, peering over my shoulder until I sent them away. They were so young I didn't fear them, and they were so fascinated by my pictures that gradually I allowed them to remain with me behind the couch. I enjoyed their attention and amazement at what I drew. When they began to ask me about the drawings, I closed my eyes and tried to speak from the place of blue light where Grandma Amana had

36

found the stories she told me when I lived with her. The children listened with wide eyes, crouching around me behind the couch as I interpreted my pictures with half-remembered tales.

Suddenly the housemother peered over the couch. She stared down at us.

"What are you doing back here? Why are you hiding?" she snapped, pulling me toward her and staring suspiciously into my face. "Oh!" she muttered. "You don't deserve it, but we have a surprise for you. It's your birthday and we have a surprise for you."

I tried to free myself from her grasp. "No . . . no," I whispered. "It is not my birthday."

"It certainly is your birthday," she insisted. "It says so right here on this index card. That's what your mother told us, and if she doesn't know I can't imagine who does! Now just be a good child and come along peacefully."

I was thrust into the dining room. There sat Reno alone at one of the tables!

"Your brother went to a lot of trouble for you, Sitko; so go sit down with him," the housemother said as she closed the door behind her, leaving me to face my brother with whom I had not spoken for many weeks.

I made my way among the tables and chairs to the center of the room where Reno sat with his hands covering a box wrapped in deep-purple paper. He did not look at me as I sat down. Then he wiped his nose and awkwardly pushed the box across the table.

"No big deal," he muttered. "But these crazy people

insist it's your birthday. They got it written down and so they got to believe it."

I stammered dreadfully, searching for words. I was so touched and happy to see him, to know he was here for me again.

"So I made something for you," he finished.

I shook my head and covered my face.

"It's nothing . . . just something I made," he said impatiently. "Open it," he murmured, self-consciously glancing away so we would not look into each other's eyes. "And stop making such a big deal out of it, for Christ's sake."

My hands trembled as I opened the gift. Under the purple paper was a beautiful wooden box with hinges and a little lock and a leather handle. I ran my hands over the wood and tried to catch my breath, but a great gust of feeling swept through me with such force, my joy and my pain collided, making me weep and laugh at the same time.

This was more than Reno could bear. He cleared his throat and fidgeted with the wrapping paper, unable to speak. Finally he touched my hands and clasped them tightly. "I made it for you, Sitko," he said. Again he cleared his throat and tears came slowly into his blue eyes. "I made it for you because you're my little brother and I'm proud of you because you can make things that are beautiful. You have something . . . something special," he murmured earnestly. "I don't know how you got it, but somehow you have this . . . this vision. And so I made this for you. It's for your crayons and colored pencils. D'you see how it opens up? And there's room inside for all the things you use when you make your pictures."

I could only gasp for breath and shake my head in amazement.

"I hope you like it," Reno said.

Still I could not speak.

"And I did something else too," Reno continued as he closed the box and pressed it into my hands. "I asked Bill to get us a bottle of Seven-Up and some vanilla ice cream. So let's get down to the eucalyptus grove before it melts and I catch hell from the housemother for dribbling it all over the place." He laughed as he pulled me after him out of the dining room and down the hall and out the door into the driving rain.

When we sat together, sheltered by the eaves of the laundry, Reno, laughing all the time, made the sodas and we drank the wonderful sweet drink while the froth and bubbles rose into our nostrils.

"Here's to us!" Reno exclaimed as he tapped his glass against mine. "That's what they call a toast!"

"Here's to us," I repeated. "To *us!*"

While we were finishing our sodas, Bill ducked out of the laundry and told us the housemother was mad as hell because we had gone out without permission.

"You two better hightail it back right now," he warned, " 'cause that housemother of yours got a terrible temper when she gets mad."

We quickly washed the glasses in the cascade streaming off the eaves, and hurried back inside.

The housemother shook her head with exasperation. "Soaked clear through and likely to get pneumonia!" she snapped. "Well, go dry yourselves and put on some clean socks and then, Sitko, I want you to go to my parlor. There's someone here to see you."

I hesitated, grasping Reno's hand. I didn't want to leave him, but the housemother reappeared at the door.

"Do as I say *at once!*"

Reno pushed me toward the door and followed me.

I rubbed my head with a towel and pulled on a dry pair of socks. I looked at Reno, hoping he would tell me I didn't have to go to the housemother's parlor. But he silently made a gesture with his head, and I saw I would have to do what I was told. I slowly climbed the stairs, glancing back to make certain Reno was following.

When I got to the top of the stairs I saw a tall, dark man standing in the doorway. He was holding a box in his hands.

I heard a groan behind me as Reno suddenly backed against the wall when he saw the man. I felt my brother grasp my shirttail, but my fascination for this man who was my father was so great that I rushed forward and stood gazing up at him.

Suddenly my father swept me up into his arms and held me close. I was overwhelmed by the strange and marvelous smell of him! He looked intently into my face, his lips twitching as if a flood of words was trying to free itself from his throat. But he said nothing. He put me down and smiled sadly at Reno, as if he fully sensed his elder son's resentment. I slowly backed away, fearing my brother's anger. Reno clutched my hand and whispered something I could not understand.

"Have you been good boys?" the man stammered, staring at Reno as if he hardly recognized the young man he had become.

Reno did not respond.

The pain in the man's face deepened. It hurt to look at him. I thought he would turn away, but he stood his ground and said falteringly, "Here . . . here . . . this is for you, Sitko. Go ahead . . . take it . . . it's for you."

I glanced at Reno but did not move.

"Take it . . . take it," Reno finally muttered under his breath, releasing me from his grasp.

I slowly approached the tall man and took the package from his large hands. "Thank you, sir," I said. I could not call him "father."

He bowed his head and then nodded apologetically to Reno. "I should have brought you something too," he whispered.

"I don't want anything from you," Reno said.

"Reno . . . you must not be angry with me . . . you are too young to understand," our father pleaded.

"I'm not mad at anybody," Reno exclaimed. "I don't care about your gifts, and I'm not angry at anybody. So just leave us alone!"

Reno turned away. "Come," he called to me. Then he started up the stairs to the dormitory. I took a step toward him, but I could not obey. I could not give up this chance of knowing the stranger who was my father.

"Sitko!" my brother shouted. "Come on right now or you'll be sorry!"

I was filled with an enormous longing to stay with my father, but I was afraid of losing Reno's love. My father would go away again, and if I lost both of them . . . I would have no one. Slowly I turned to follow Reno.

Then all at once my father took me by the shoulders and would not let me go.

"Don't be afraid, Sitko," he said gently. "I must talk to you. You're such a little fellow you can't understand all of this, but you have to try to listen to me because I'm your father and I love you. Are you listening to me, Sitko?" he entreated with such intensity that I was filled with pain for him.

"Sitko!" Reno shouted.

I pulled against my father's grasp, trembling with confusion, but he would not let me go. He held me tightly as he began to speak quickly in an anxious voice. "I don't want you to spend your childhood in a place like this. You need to have a family that loves you. Do you understand? It's different for Reno. He won't be here much longer, because in a couple more years he'll be out of school and have a job. But what will become of you then, Sitko? What will become of you?" my father repeated as he took both my hands and pressed them to his chest. "So . . . you see . . . your mother . . . she wants you to have a home of your own. She wants you to have a new daddy who can give you a home. He's a good man, Sitko. I've known him for a long, long time, and he promised me he would be very good to you. He has a big house with lots of land and a little guest house where all of us lived for a while—do you remember?—and I know that he will love you and give you the things I can't. Do you understand, Sitko, do you understand?"

I shook my head violently at the thought of being given away to somebody I did not remember. "No . . . no . . . no," I cried, pulling away harder.

"Oh God, try to understand, Sitko! If Alex doesn't do this then somebody else will take you and you won't be able to see us anymore! Don't you see what I'm trying to say to you, Sitko?" he exclaimed in a hoarse voice. "He wants to give you his name because he doesn't have a family of his own. He wants you to live with him in his big house because he doesn't have a wife and he doesn't have any children. He wants to be your father, Sitko. Dear God, I don't want to do this, but if I don't . . . then we'll never see you again! You'll be stuck in the Home, and anybody will be able to take you! Anybody!"

I watched in dread as my father's voice was swallowed up in his chest and he sank to his knees before me, covering his face with his large hands, and shaking with stifled sobs. Reno howled and ran up the stairs, his hands reaching desperately out into empty space. I backed away in fear, just as the housemother came. She quietly took me by the hand, and as she led me away down the long hall, I twisted around so I could see the tall, dark man sobbing on his knees.

Five

━ ━ ━ ━ ━ ━ ━

"I want you to tell your brother to stop telling all those lies to the other children or I'll send him to the headmaster," the housemother told Reno.

Reno had never looked so strong and handsome. "Never mind about Sitko," he said defiantly. "Leave him alone. Give him back his crayons or I'll write my mother!"

"And what do you think your mother can do about it?" the housemother said with an unpleasant grin. "She doesn't even come to see you! And she doesn't pay a cent toward your keep. So you mind what you say, Reno Ghost Horse, or you'll find yourself in real trouble."

"And you just leave my brother alone!" he persisted angrily. "He hasn't done anything wrong, but you're always picking on him!"

"Picking on him?" the woman exclaimed impatiently. "How dare you say such a thing! Your brother can hardly speak English. He's always somewhere that he shouldn't be, making those pictures day in and day out! He's so far behind in school that Miss Hill has given up on him.

He tells terrible stories to the children and scares them
to death so they can't sleep at night. And you're trying
to tell me that I pick on him! Well, you just listen to
me, young man: You and your brother are charity cases
in a public institution! That's right . . . charity cases! And
if your brother weren't so impossible, believe me, we
would have had him adopted and out of here long ago.
So you just go up to the dormitory and stay there until
you learn how to behave!"

It didn't matter how often they made Reno go to bed
or how often he had to do extra chores, he wouldn't
allow anyone to mistreat me.

Now Reno sat sullenly on his bed while I gazed up
at him with adoration and gratitude.

"Damn old witch," he grunted angrily. "Damn old
witch!"

I took his hand, but he pulled away.

"And you're not much better," he said. "Always acting
crazy and getting me in trouble! Geez, Sitko, I don't
know why the hell you can't be like the other kids. I'm
always getting into scraps over you. If it's not the housemother, it's the other guys. And if it keeps up, pretty
soon I won't have any friends."

I was crushed. But when I tried to back away from
him, he took me by the shoulders and sighed. "Now
don't you go get worked up. Christ's sake, I'm trying to
help you, Sitko. The least you could do is try to be a
little more . . . y'know, a little more like a regular person."

I looked at my brother solemnly and said, "I will try,

Reno. I'll try. I won't make any more pictures and I won't tell any more stories and I'll try, Reno, really I'll try to be so regular that the boys will like me. I'll be so regular that even Wilma will like me!"

To my surprise and delight Reno laughed. Suddenly he smiled and laughed and shook me gently by the shoulders as he looked at me with affection. "You're a nut . . . that's what you are, Sitko . . . a nut. But don't worry about the housemother or the boys or Wilma. It's bad enough that I have to worry about her." He laughed. "And I don't want you to give up your pictures neither. But I don't want you to scare the other kids with those stories of yours. And I want you to try harder in school and I want you to try not to make the other guys so mad at you. Okay? Is that a promise?"

I hugged my brother, closing my eyes and pressing myself to him. "Yes . . . yes . . . I promise, Reno. I promise."

But I didn't know how to be a regular person. I watched the other children, but I couldn't understand why I was different from them. I tried to imitate them when they played and when they spoke, but something always went wrong, and I couldn't bear their ridicule when I failed.

The children my own age had given me up long ago. There was no way I could win their admiration or friendship. The only kids I played with were the very young children, and I towered over them like a gangly giant. They still lived in their imaginations, and they were entranced by my pictures and my stories. And so, when I wasn't drawing, I would collect them around me and tell the stories Grandma Amana used to tell.

"One day . . ." I whispered, "one golden day Old Man went out hunting and took Brother Fox with him for company. Well, they hunted for several days without catching a single thing. After a while, they came upon a herd of buffalo, and Old Man said, 'My friend, Mr. Fox, I can think of only one way to get close enough to those buffalo to kill one for our dinner. You must allow me to pluck out all the fur on your body except for a tiny little tuft on the very end of your bushy tail. Then you have to go over to the other hill—way over there— and walk up and down in full view of the buffalo. Surely they will think that you are so funny that they will laugh themselves to death!' Brother Fox did not like the idea of having all his beautiful fur plucked out, but he was exceedingly hungry, and he finally agreed to do what Old Man suggested. So Old Man plucked and plucked until poor Mr. Fox was completely bare, except for one little fluffy tuft right at the end of his bushy tail. Then Fox hurried over to the hill and began strutting up and down and up and down. Well, when those buffalo got a look at Mr. Fox, they stood up on their feet and gazed in astonishment at one another. They didn't know what to make of this crazy-looking creature on top of the hill. Then, as they saw Brother Fox waving his skinny little tufted tail back and forth they began to smile. The more they watched the more they laughed. Mr. Fox took advantage of the situation, and he began to do the most ridiculous things. He stood on his head and he shook his fluffy little tail straight up in the air. He tiptoed on all four feet with his tail wiggling to and fro. Well, the more tricks he did the harder all the buffalo laughed, until one by one they dropped stone-cold dead of excessive merriment!"

The children began to giggle. But then I was overcome by the blue light that glows in the place where the stories live. I felt far away from the children, seized by something strange and remote. "The Fox is powerful," I whispered. "So do not laugh too hard at him if you value your lives. He is funny, but in his foolishness there is great power!"

The children became silent. They peered fearfully at each other and glanced cautiously over their shoulders.

"I know the Fox," I whispered. "I have talked to him at night when he comes to me. He teaches me things. He shows me the scenes I paint. He stands up next to my bed on two feet. His bushy coat turns red with fire and burns like a torch. It is then he teaches me strange, lost things."

Reno suddenly peered over the couch and the children, terrified, screamed and scattered. I looked up into Reno's troubled face.

"You must not frighten the children, or the housemother will make trouble for us, Sitko. You promised you'd try to stay out of trouble and act like the other kids. You promised!"

Something strange and powerful was still happening inside me.

"You'll be punished by God if you keep telling those stories," Reno said. "It's true. All I'm telling you is true.

God is more powerful than your fox, and God is going
to punish you for breaking your promise to me!"

I shook my head slowly, ignoring Reno's anger. There
was something terrifying and powerful within me. I gazed
silently at my brother. I stared over his shoulder at
something that floated just beyond him . . . something
terrible that he could not see. My gaze frightened Reno.
He swallowed hard and said, "You're crazy, Sitko!" And
then he quickly left without daring to look back over
his shoulder for fear of seeing what it was that I could
see in the vast darkness that surrounded our lives.

Six

I told beautiful stories, but the housemother said I was a liar, and Reno said I was crazy. Now the stories dried up and were gone.

I had made a Chinese garden, but before it grew, someone had pulled up the trellises. Nothing remained of my garden. The sweet peas had suffocated under the dark earth. I dreamed about the fragile sprouts trapped within the seeds, unable to grow. I dreamed of the seeds slowly dying, lost forever in the soil where they had forgotten the blossoms hidden deep within themselves. All this I dreamed. And then I cried out and awakened, staring fearfully into the darkness of the dormitory. Night after night I dreamed about the Chinese garden, until at last I too was suffocating under the heavy folds of earth. I was trapped within myself. I could not sprout or bloom.

I screamed into the night, tearing away the sheets that confined me and rushing into the vast breathless darkness of the dormitory. I fought against the hands that restrained me. I kicked and bit and gasped for breath as the sky enveloped me. I groaned up at the Moon as she swallowed all the stars and smiled her evil silvery smile. Then suddenly she laughed and pushed me over the brink, and I fell headlong into myself.

It was in the night of the dying stars that they sent me to the doctor's office.

Reno took my hand and led me away, while I heard owls whispering. Reno led me to the bungalow where the doctor had his office. We sat there silently—side by side, but utterly remote from one another. I could see the panic and embarrassment in my brother's eyes. But I had stepped into a world where he could not follow. His eyes looked at me across an abyss filled with all that is unnamed and unknown.

When the doctor finally came muttering along in his bathrobe, Reno got up and left me without saying a word. I gazed after my brother, from my own world, haunted by the expression in his eyes. I felt a jab in my arm, and before I could cry out in pain, I slipped out of the doctor's grasp and plummeted like a star into the dusty mouth of the silver Moon.

"It's unnatural . . . heplayswithchildrenmuchyoungerthanheis," I heard.

Far over my head I could see the housemother, drifting to and fro, her mouth moving and her eyes blinking mechanically like a baby doll's. I tried to follow her words, but they were jumbled and shrill.

I wanted to get up, but I could not reach the opening above me where a dim light glowed. I could not climb out of the suffocating blackness that surrounded me. In the distance I could hear water trickling. I could hear voices. I could feel hands touching me, hurting me. And I knew that I would die from all the shots and the needles and the knives doctors use in hospitals. I would die and then they would carry me away on a stretcher. And people I had never known would walk beside my body very slowly, wearing black and paying twenty-five cents to look at me.

"How extraordinary!"

"How very brown he is!"

"I've never seen anybody so brown!"

"How coarse and ugly his hair is!"

"I never saw hair like that!"

"He tells lies," the nurse was saying. "He doesn't seem to distinguish between truth and fantasy."

"Is that right?" the doctor asked, approaching me with a little flat stick that he pushed abruptly into my mouth. I choked and could not answer him. "Do you tell lies? Is that what you do?"

"The housemother can't handle him," the nurse continued. "And the brother is too protective."

"Is that right?" the doctor said, opening my pajama shirt and pressing a cold, silver disk against my chest. "Do you tell lots of lies? Is that what you've been doing, young man?"

"He doesn't make friends, and the other children resent him. He tells them that his father is in the rodeo and that his grandmother has magical powers . . . all kinds of crazy things."

"Is that what you've been telling the other children?" the doctor muttered as he stuck something into my ears and into my nose. "Don't you know that little boys get punished for telling lies? Don't you know that liars go to hell when they die?"

"No! No!" I shouted, leaping to my feet and running for the door.

I began to scream as they chased me. I began to shout as loudly as I could shout. I rushed through the halls and out into the street where the owls peered at me and hooted.

"No! No!" I shouted.

I was blinded by tears that streamed down my face. I could not see, but still I could not stop running. I fell down again and again, getting up and feeling my arms and knees sting with pain as I rushed in search of Reno, hoping he would protect me, praying that he would hide me.

Then suddenly I crashed into someone. When I peered up, I saw the headmaster glaring down at me.

I sat on my bed in the dormitory, looking out the window at the children on the playground. The tray from the dining room had not been taken away for two days. The food smelled sour. Reno had not come to see me. None of the other boys were allowed to speak to me, and I was told I would be punished if I spoke to them. When the housemother came through the door at the far end of the dormitory, I ran into the lavatory and hid in one of the stalls, locking the door behind me.

"You come out of there, Sitko, if you know what's good for you! I've had enough of this nonsense!" the housemother shouted.

But I would not answer and I would not come out.

I waited anxiously, listening to her footsteps as she went away.

After a long time, when it began to get dark, I heard someone come into the lavatory. I peered through the crack in the door. It was Reno.

"Reno! Reno!"

For a moment there was no reply. Then my brother said: "You're going to get in a whole lot of trouble if you don't come out, Sitko! D'you hear me?"

"But they'll punish me," I wailed helplessly. "They'll hit me!"

"They promised me they won't punish you if you come out right now and behave yourself," Reno said in a stern voice. "But you've got to come out now, d'you hear?"

"Promise me! Promise me, Reno, that they won't hurt me," I pleaded.

"I already told you they won't punish you if you do what I say."

"Do you swear to it, Reno? Do you really swear to it?"

There was no response. I waited, but Reno said nothing. I was afraid, but the sound of my brother's breathing comforted me. I was certain that he wouldn't let anything terrible happen to me. And so I decided to unlock the door. But when I peeked out, the bathroom was deserted. Reno had vanished.

"Reno!" I shouted. But there was no reply.

I listened carefully, and then I cautiously unlatched the door and crept out. No sooner had I stepped into the dark dormitory than someone seized me by the hair and dragged me to my bed.

It was the headmaster. I shuddered with fear. He stared down at me, and then he began to strike me again and again with a stick. My body burned as the headmaster shouted and beat me. My limbs winced and quivered each time the stick struck my flesh. Blood started to run out of my nostrils. I screamed and begged him to stop. Blood spurted from my mouth and I could not see. My stomach rolled upward and I choked on my vomit. But still he beat me. Now I could no longer feel the blows. A long warm wave rolled slowly over me and I felt myself falling to the floor. I could not see, but I could hear the headmaster shouting—cursing and shouting as he continued to beat me. I groaned and reached toward him for mercy. Then the stick struck my arm with terrible force, and I heard the bone shatter and burst. I felt my skin split and open up as the ragged splinters of my bone pushed slowly out of my flesh. A ferocious pain took hold of me, shaking me violently until I could no longer breathe. The world was sliding away from me. The owls hooted and the Moon laughed as two thousand stars died in her mouth. Then slowly the Fox crept out of my broken body and disappeared under the bed.

At last it was silent.

When I awakened my arm was covered with white plaster, and I was strapped into the bed. I could not move, and my face was so bruised that I was unable to speak.

The nurse peered down at me when she heard my groans, but she did not speak. A moment later the face of the headmaster appeared above me and I shuddered with fear. He looked at me without expression, and then, satisfied that I was alive, he went away. The light went out, and I was alone again.

Three weeks later the man called Alexander Miller came to see me. The headmaster smiled at me and patted me on the head. "This is your new father," he said as the nurse released the straps and helped me sit up.

I was flooded with dizziness as I heard the headmaster add, "It looks worse than it is."

The nurse smiled as she dressed me, sending torrents of pain through my limbs each time she touched my bruises. "The boys play so hard," she was saying to the friend of my father named Alexander Miller, "it's a wonder they don't kill themselves. Fortunately their little bones mend quickly."

I peered at them through my swollen eyelids, mumbling but unable to speak.

"Believe me," the headmaster was saying, "the boys who did this have been severely punished."

He pulled me after him and led me downstairs to a white room. On the table was a box containing my belongings.

I winced as the headmaster stooped down and looked into my face. "Do you understand, child? Do you understand that you're going home with this nice gentleman? You're going to his beautiful house. Do you understand?"

I drew back from the headmaster and whimpered. I still could not move my lips without dreadful pain. Alexander Miller held out his hand to me. I looked about me and sobbed out of my helplessness. I didn't want to go with this man, but I feared the headmaster so much that I hesitantly took Alexander Miller's hand and followed him down the steps.

Alexander Miller was talking, but I could not understand what he was saying. I was filled with dread and hopelessness as I was led into an immense and strange world. I had no voice. I had no defenses against the loneliness and helplessness that had overtaken me. I longed for Grandma Amana, but she had vanished. I hung my head as I was led away from Star of Good Hope . . . as we passed the dormitory where Reno and I had lived . . . the white house of the headmaster, the fountain where the boy and girl huddled beneath their green umbrella, and beyond the white line that we were forbidden to cross. We went down the narrow road, past the laundry and the grove of eucalyptus trees, and out the gate by the railroad tracks. And when the train came, we got into one of the wooden cars and, while I silently peered out the window, trying to understand the confusion and torment I felt, we began to move farther and farther away from the Star of Good Hope, until at last it had vanished into the gray haze that rose from the wide, honey-colored plains.

Seven

━ ━ ━ ━ ━ ━ ━ ━ ━

"I*ss-sa! Hai-yak!* . . . What have they done to you?"
Grandma Amana exclaimed when I stumbled into
the house. "What have those people done to you? *Kai-
yay-wah?* What have they done to your face and arm,
my little one?" she wailed as she drew me away from
Alexander Miller, despite his objections, and rushed me
into the kitchen.

"*E-spoom-mo-kin-on!* . . . Help us survive these people! Help us!" she wept as she bathed my face with salt
water and peered in disbelief at the casket of stone in
which they had buried my arm. She stared at me and
then drew a great breath to give her strength. A slow
smile transformed her old face. "Now you are safe," she
murmured, gazing at me with so much love in her eyes
that I fell into the warmth of her arms, enveloped in
the marvelous smell of rich brown earth.

"Ah," she intoned as she rocked me in her embrace,
"now you are safe . . . now you are truly safe."

In her magical arms, I felt the pain instantly vanish

59

from my limbs. The terror withdrew from my spirit, flying away with a frantic flapping of wings. My voice came back into my throat, and the whirlpool within my troubled mind changed into a deep dark river of memories.

"*E-spoom-mo-kin-on!*" I whispered, the lost words reforming on my lips. "Grandma Amana," I whispered again and again, fearful that her warm protective arms might vanish.

"*Aih,* do you see what your mother has done with us?" she chanted quietly. "She has put us in the guest house of this man . . . this Alexander Miller. He has taken us away from your father. He has taken all of us . . . like pets to play with . . . like dogs that follow at his heels," she softly complained. "With his money he has bought the family of Jamie Ghost Horse. That is what this friend . . . this so-called friend of your father has done."

Suddenly Alexander Miller burst into the kitchen, followed anxiously by my mother. He was shouting.

"You tell her right now!" he was yelling. "Tell her right now!"

"Sitko! Sitko!" my mother cried as she pulled me from the arms of Grandma Amana. "Just look at how you have grown! Just look at my big boy!"

I stood there trembling. My mother wept and my grandmother groaned and Alexander Miller screamed, "Jemina, I want you should tell her what I said. . . . I want you should tell her she's not going to spoil this kid with a lot of nonsense . . . not in my house she isn't. 'Cause I won't put up with her meddling! No sooner do

I bring him home, she takes him over! But she's not having her way! Not while I'm paying the bills!" he shouted, pulling me away from my grandmother, the pain from his grasp bringing back the agony in my body. "You wanted to have your mother and your kid here. . . . Well, okay . . . so now you have them. But he's going to speak English like the other kids, and he's going to grow up to be an American and nothing else but an American! So I want you should tell her that that's the way it's going to be or believe me I'll tell her!"

"Stop it," Jemina pleaded. "The poor child has been in the hospital. So for heaven's sake, Alex, stop it."

My mother led me out of the kitchen. We climbed the staircase of the guest house and finally came to a door which Jemina opened. Inside was the most beautiful room I had ever seen. The walls were paneled with polished wood. There was a thick rug on the floor, and the drawers and closets were built into the walls and covered with maroon leather. But the most wonderful thing about this room was the huge bed, built so high I would have to climb a ladder in order to get into it. On each side of the immense bed were long draperies with Mexican peasants embroidered on them in bright colored threads. And there was on the bed itself a handsome quilt of elkskin.

My mother gently pressed me forward onto the thick rug.

"This is your room, Sitko," she whispered as tears came into her eyes. "This is going to be your bedroom."

I looked up at my mother in confusion.

"Go ahead, dear. It's all right. Go inside . . . because now this is your room."

I took a few steps, peering in amazement at the electric clock on the little desk. I touched the crisp white curtains that framed the sunlit windows. I carefully climbed the ladder and put one hand on the immense bed. And then I turned to my mother. She was weeping. She was weeping and smiling as she looked up at me. Then suddenly she hurried from the room.

I waited for her or grandmother to come for me, but there was no sound in the house except the distant, grumbling voice of Alexander Miller and the sound of Grandma Amana's chanting.

I slipped onto the great, soft bed, and felt as though I had been given the highest place in the sky in which to sleep. I closed my eyes.

"*I-yo-ka*," I murmured. "Sleep."

In the summer days the orchard that surrounded the guest house of Alexander Miller was filled with the drone of insects and the chatter of birds. The warm sun gradually healed my bruises, and eventually the cast was removed from my arm. My fingers were still too weak to hold a crayon, and though I wanted to draw what I saw in this new world, I had to content myself with looking at the beauty of the summer days.

In the evening the mockingbirds sang to one another across the vast fields of golden grass and hollyhocks. And by day, Grandma Amana and I sat happily under the cloudless sky. She sang softly and cut vegetables for dinner, slowly turning string beans and potatoes in her wrinkled brown hands. I gazed up at the great house on the hill where Alexander Miller lived. I was forbidden to go there, but once I slipped through the bushes and peeked into a window, hoping to see my mother.

I rarely saw her because she often stayed in the big house. Every time she left us, Grandma Amana would sigh heavily, watching after her with a sad expression.

"You have abandoned your husband and taken up with this foreigner," my grandmother whispered angrily when my mother was leaving.

Before she could say more, my mother would gesture toward me. "We can talk about this later," she said, giving my grandmother a dark look. "The child has enough problems without hearing this. But let me remind you, Mother, that it was Jamie Ghost Horse who abandoned me!"

At night, when I went to bed, Grandma Amana prayed that my father would come back and take us away to a house of our own. Sometimes my mother came into my bedroom and stood silently in the darkness. I could hear her breathing and watched as she paced back and forth and wept.

I pretended that I was asleep. But I could not sleep while my mother wept and the house was filled with my grandmother's chanting.

The Moon peered into my dreams and blinked her great white eyes and laughed. *"Your agony will not end,"* she whispered. *"It follows after you and sinks its teeth into your heart."*

I tried to wish away her terrible white face, but still the Moon laughed and whispered into my ear.

When the summer ended, I was taken by Alexander Miller to the local school.

"His name is Seymour Miller," he lied. "Sometimes they call him Sitko. He has some funny ideas, but he's a good boy, and I know you'll look after him for us."

Then he turned and left me in the playground.

The children circled me slowly, staring at me. I knew at once that they did not like me. I lifted my hand toward them, but they drew back, refusing my friendship. I desperately wanted to be liked. But I didn't know how to make friends with them. I realized that if I let them retreat from me this time, I would be lost forever in myself. And so I summoned my courage and stammered: "My name is Sitko Ghost Horse. I want to be your friend."

They stared at me. Then one boy began to laugh.

"Sitko Ghost Horse!" he mocked. "You've got to be kidding!"

Then they all began to laugh and ran away, leaving me alone in the middle of the deserted playground.

The road leading to the house of Alexander Miller waited for me each afternoon as I dashed in flight from the children who followed me home from school singing, *"Ghost Horsey . . . Ghost Horsey!"*

I didn't tell Grandma Amana about the way I was treated because it humiliated me to admit that once again all the children at school made fun of me. I could not understand why my mother dressed me up for school so I looked like a sissy. I begged her to let me wear jeans like the other boys, but she would not listen.

"For once in our lives we are going to dress like real people, Sitko. Not like trash but like decent folks. So let's not hear any more complaining. Those kids just envy you because you have such nice things."

So I stayed close to Grandma Amana, venturing only hesitantly into the spacious grounds surrounding the house of Alexander Miller. I stayed in the kitchen and listened to my grandmother tell her stories of the old days. We had lived somewhere far away . . . where people were as beautiful as eagles. She told me about the days when our people were free and strong.

"We had many horses and we were strong . . . oh, so very strong!" Grandma Amana murmured as she peeled potatoes. "We had so many good things."

"But . . . we don't have many good things anymore," I said.

"*Aih*, that's right. We have nothing. Even the *oo-kon* is gone; even the Sun Dance Medicine Lodge is gone now."

I watched my grandmother as her eyes filled with memories. Her face was as wrinkled and brown as a turtle's. She seemed like the oldest person in the world, but her wonderful dark eyes shone with power and youth.

She dropped a potato into the water, and it made a big splash, so we laughed.

"*Oo-ne-ke* . . . Milk . . . You drink your milk, and I will tell you how it is that we came to have nothing," she said. "I will tell you about the last great days of our grandfathers and how they died with the Moon and the Stars upon their chests."

And then Grandma Amana drew in her breath, and a blue light appeared within her body as she sat in the kitchen peeling potatoes and dropping them one by one into the big pot of water. She closed her eyes to summon the story from within her body, and then she began to chant.

"One day, when the *na-pe-koo-wan* . . . the strangers . . . were still few and the grass did not know their feet and the land did not know their hands, there were many animals and many good things of the earth for all to eat. The animals were our friends and our teachers, giving us the wisdom which turns the earth green and brings rain and sunshine. These were the good days. But the grass began to die and the animals no longer spoke to us. The land was filled with strangers, and there were no more good days for us. The wind stirs the willows. Fog! Lightning! Whirlwind! The rocks are ringing, they are ringing from the tall mountains. Now the Sun's yellow beams are running out. Great Sun is dying in the west. But we shall live again. We shall live again!"

Eight

▬ ▬ ▬ ▬ ▬ ▬ ▬ ▬

It was in the time of the lightning and whirlwind that I came back to Grandma Amana.

I wandered out into the wild flowers, venturing through the sea of tall grass that the wind had brushed into wide, sloping waves. At the bottom of the black walnut grove I paused apprehensively, looking down the road that led to the school where the children's voices rose from the playground. They had shut me out from their merriment. And so I turned away and sat among the trimmed hedges and the rows of marigolds. And I dreamed of my Chinese garden—a mass of tall green vines rising from the rich black soil, two thousand blossoms turning many colors in the sunlight, where unicorns bathed in a crimson pool beneath a pagoda, and peacocks slowly opened their emerald tails.

On the hill was the great house of Alexander Miller. I looked at it from a distance, hoping to see my mother. But she was rarely home.

Grandma Amana complained each time my mother

packed her suitcase and waited by the door of our guest house for Alexander Miller's automobile.

"Mother!" she whispered under her breath, hoping that I would not understand. "I have a right to have friends . . . so just stop it!"

"If he is such a good friend," my grandmother answered, "then why doesn't he make you his wife?"

Jemina frowned with anger.

"Isn't it enough that he adopted Sitko? Isn't it enough that he put this house in your name so you'll always have a place to live? What do you want from him, Mama!"

"I want him to stay away from the wife of Jamie Ghost Horse, that is what I want!" my grandmother replied.

"Mama, I'm going . . . please let's not argue. The car is here. I have to leave. Give me a kiss and try to understand that I'm doing the best I can for all of us."

My grandmother nodded dolefully as Jemina kissed her lightly on her wrinkled cheek. "He has taken your child, but he doesn't want you," she muttered as my mother hurried away.

No matter how often Jemina told me that Alexander Miller was my father, I knew it was not true. I was a borrowed child of that other, tall father who had come to me at the Home. Even the garden was only a borrowed garden that belonged to someone else. When Alexander Miller told me to come to the big house, I knew that he was only being nice to my mother but he didn't like me. When he kissed me, the kiss was never for me, but for her. When he bought me things, they were never things I wanted, but things he wanted me to want. And when he took me to the place where he worked or when he took me to the golf course, he told people that I was his real son, although I was the son of another man—a tall, dark man who had disappeared.

Alexander Miller called me Sy, because he said that Sitko wasn't a good name. He told me that he worked in the movies and that his professional name was Hilton instead of Miller, even though Grandma Amana told me his real name was Milas. He said that I was to call him "Father." And when I forgot, he became angry and shouted at my mother.

I was uncertain about everything. The things other children took for granted about themselves and their families were mysteries to me: where and when I was born and to whom I truly belonged. I asked about these things, but always my mother and grandmother gave me different answers; so my confusion grew.

"Stop thinking about the past," my mother insisted. "You have a new family. The past doesn't matter."

But it mattered to me. Without it I wasn't anybody. I didn't know who I was. When I searched my mind for people and places, I could find just fragments, shadowy faces, landscapes without names, events out of time. I was not certain which things I remembered and which I had been told. Even my birthday was a mystery to me, though the housemother at the Home insisted on celebrating it. And gradually I began to realize that there were two realities: the one that existed between my mother and grandmother, and another reality that existed between my mother and Alexander Miller. Both of these realities blended into a fragmented world where I could not find the truth.

Whatever I said to Alexander Miller seemed to cause trouble. "Where is Reno?" I asked. "Where is my father?"

"I'm your father, damn it!" Alexander exclaimed. "Do you hear what I'm telling you? I'm your father!"

Then they argued. Later my mother scolded me. "I told you to be quiet about Reno and Jamie."

"But Mother . . ." I protested.

"No buts about it, young man. Do you understand me?"

Alexander and Jemina were always quarreling.

"I want to learn this kid something," he told my mother. "But your mother keeps filling his head with all that Indian nonsense. It's no wonder he can't even talk good English."

My mother and Alexander would begin to shout at one another. Their loud voices frightened me, so I ran back to Grandma Amana in the guest house. But their angry voices trailed after me through the dark.

"Believe me," Alexander Miller shouted, "I don't need to be loaded down with somebody else's kid! I don't care if Jamie was a friend of mine! I don't owe him anything! I'm just a damn fool for letting you talk me into this!"

Even in my sleep I could hear my mother and Alexander Miller shouting at each other.

I awakened in dread, afraid of my dreams and fearful of awakening to the real world, real children, real school. I had no friends, and within myself I had no history;

there was only confusion, strange, unconfirmed memories. My only sanctuary was the garden where I sat alone among the flowers or climbed the great oak tree and sat for hours among the leafy branches listening to other people. In the evening, the San Fernando Valley was filled with the sounds of families . . . of children and their fathers and mothers, of silverware and platters, radios and music. I longed to be part of such a home. I wanted to be a child like other children, but I was closed off from them by mysteries I did not understand.

Except for a few poor farmers, almost everyone in the Valley worked in the motion-picture business. Here and there, between the big houses with their circular driveways full of automobiles, were the wooden bungalows of the farmers. They were pale people—with white hair and blank eyes that dolefully watched as newcomers took over the land that had been settled by their ancestors. Their children were as pale as they were: blond hair, light blue, vacant eyes, and skin so white it seemed as if it would bruise if it were touched.

Larry was such a child, the son of farmers who had once owned a big spread in the Valley. Now they had a few acres where they kept some chickens and a goat named Millie. Larry was not very smart in school, and the rich kids called him the Jolly Green Giant because he was tall and the knees of his jeans were always stained with grass. Nobody particularly liked Larry, but he seemed like a gentle boy, and I hoped he might be my friend.

Eventually we got to know each other, and after school we would hike through the empty lots, talking about animals and airplanes. And so Larry and I became friends.

Now no one taunted me anymore. The two of us, as we romped through the foxtails, were a fierce-looking pair. Larry was even taller than I, but instead of being skinny he was a big fellow.

I wanted to ask Larry to come to my house, but Jemina and Alexander didn't like me to have anything to do with the farmers' kids. And Larry never asked me to come over to his house. So the two of us just wandered around and talked until it started getting dark, and then we'd hurry home.

One day Larry and I were hiking down toward the creek where Grandma Amana sometimes went to gather watercress. It was a beautiful place, a wide, shallow river-bed where the floodwater swept in a surging, deep stream during cloudbursts. But in the summer and fall the creek narrowed into a delicate stream of clear, rushing water that cut deeply into the gray and red clay, and then widened into little pools where frogs and crayfish lived beneath the thick beds of watercress.

The creek was lined by the shallow land still owned by farmers. It often flooded in the rainy season, so the rich people were afraid to build near the creek. The farmers happily kept the land for themselves.

As Larry and I hiked through the willows and splashed into the shallow pools, we could hear chickens cackling and a few cows mooing to be milked. The farmers were in their little gardens, and some of them waved to Larry. But he never took me to visit any of them.

"That's our place over there," Larry said, as we edged

across a wide vegetable patch filled with corn and to-matoes.

Then a big man suddenly appeared, coming out of a toolshed and catching sight of us. Larry looked fright-ened.

"Hey, boy!" the man shouted. "You come on in here right now or you'll get it good! How many times do I have to tell you to stay away from that damn pachuco kid!"

"I gotta go. . . . I gotta go right now," Larry stam-mered as he ran toward his house.

"You get!" the man shouted as he threw a clod of dirt at me. "You just go play with your own kind!" he yelled as he strode toward me with his shovel in hand.

I bolted and ran as fast as I could run.

"It ain't bad enough we got a whole load of Jews 'round here," the man shouted. "We got to get a bunch of wetbacks on top of it!"

When I had run far into the middle of the creek and was out of the angry man's reach, I suddenly stopped and turned around, raising both of my arms into the air, and to my amazement I began to shout as loud as I could. "I'm not a Mexican, you dumb sonofabitch! Do you hear me? I said I'm not a Mexican! My father is a bareback rider and he's better than you are and he's bigger than you are! Do you hear me! I'm not a Mexican! I'm an American Indian! Do you hear me, you old bas-tard! I'm an American Indian! And if you don't like it, you can go screw yourself!"

Then I began to run as fast as my long, skinny legs

could carry me. And as I ran, I felt so utterly marvelous that I began to roar with laughter. Tears of joy ran across my face. The sky opened up to me, grinning its sunny smile. And I felt better than I had ever felt in my whole life.

In the evenings I sat in a corner of the kitchen under Grandma Amana's gaze, making pictures. I was thinking of the emerald peacocks and the misty pool of my Chinese garden . . . brilliant bursts of color in golden sunlight . . . water rippling and leaping . . . flowers and animals dissolving into a river of rainbows. I tried again and again to draw the marvelous images inside my mind, but I could not get them down on paper. Finally, I threw down my crayons and tore up my sketches.

"Do not be in such a hurry," Grandma Amana murmured over her pots and pans. "Nothing can be born until it is ready."

I shook my head with frustration while my grandmother picked up the crayons and placed them back on the table. "Don't be afraid of failure, Sitko. You can learn nothing if you are unwilling to make mistakes."

"But I can't do it! I want to make a picture, but I can't draw the things I see!"

Grandma Amana smiled and gave me a glass of milk and crackers. Then she laboriously reached into her apron and from her money pouch she took out seventy-five cents. "Maybe it will be easier if you get some water paints," she said. "Maybe the things you see want to be made of water paints instead of crayons."

I hugged her exuberantly, knowing that she was not just giving me a present. Her gift to me was the freedom to find myself and to express my visions as a true artist. It was as if she were saying: *I believe in you, Sitko!*

Snatching the coins, I ran joyously out to find Larry so we could go to Woolworth's before it closed.

I hid in the willows in the creek and made our secret call: barking like a dog three times. In a moment, Larry hurried out of the toolshed and loped toward me.

"Sure," he said, "I'll go with you! You got enough money? Them watercolor sets cost a lot of money, Sy."

Larry was right. When I found the watercolor set I really wanted, I realized I didn't have enough money.

"Can't you use your allowance?" Larry asked. "Can't you do a few more chores and ask for a little more allowance?"

"What's an allowance?"

"Don't you get something for working around your house?"

I had to bring the garbage cans in from the curb and wash them out with the green hose in the garden, and I had to weed the parkways every Saturday morning and trim the grass around the sprinklers on the lawn by the big house, but I had never been given any money.

"Heck," Larry exclaimed, "what kind of dad do you have, anyway? He's supposed to give you an allowance! Everybody I know gets an allowance."

I looked with embarrassment at my friend.

"He must be some kind of awful piker," Larry said.

"It's just like my pa always says—those movie people are a bunch of kikes."

"What's a kike?" I asked.

"Y'know . . . one of them Jewish people . . . one of them hymies."

"But . . . Alexander isn't a hymie," I denied, fearful that I had discovered yet another reason that people would disapprove of me.

"Maybe not . . . but his name is Miller, isn't it? And my pa says that if your name is Miller then you gotta be a Jew. He had you figured to be a Mexican, but when I told him your name's Sy Miller, he said sure enough you gotta be a hymie."

I looked at Larry with apprehension, fearing that Jews were bad people. If he believed I was a Jew he might not want to be my friend anymore.

"I don't hold it against you, Sy," he said, reading the concern in my face. "But your father is a kike, and that's why he's so miserly he doesn't even give you an allowance."

"That isn't how it is, Larry. You see, my real father . . ." I started to explain. But then I was ashamed to confess that my real father was not Alexander Miller but Jamie Ghost Horse. I didn't want to admit that my father had given me to another man. So I didn't know what to say.

Larry shrugged and nodded fondly in an expression of sympathy. Then his eyes lit up with an idea, and he suddenly started fishing in his pockets.

"Here," he said. "I got a dollar and sixty-three cents!

You just take it, see, and then you can give it back when you get some money from your dad."

I swallowed hard and gazed at the money in Larry's hand. Grandma Amana's understanding, Larry's kindness overwhelmed me.

"Geez, Sy, you gotta have this paint set if you're ever gonna be a great painter; so just borrow the money and you can always give it back. After all, what are friends for?"

Filled with joy at the double gift of love this day, I accepted the money, and with it I was able to purchase a splendid set of watercolors . . . twelve different colors and six mink brushes in a beautiful metal box. I was filled with an immense love for my friend as we walked out of Woolworth's. But I didn't know how to thank him. I wanted to explain everything to him. I wanted to tell him that Alexander Miller was not my real father. I wanted to tell him that my name was Sitko Ghost Horse. I wanted Larry to close his eyes so he could see the Fox and the land in the north which still lingered in my memory. But I had never spoken of these secrets since the day that Freddy and Suzie had betrayed me. I could not find the words to tell Larry the truth. I didn't know what to do with the overwhelming feeling of gratitude I felt toward him. I simply nudged him on the shoulder and smiled into his face.

"Geez," he laughed self-consciously, "you're even loonier than I am, Sy!" Then we raced each other to the little wooden bridge that crossed high above the creek. There we parted without a word.

That night I sat in the kitchen with my watercolors, delighted by the fluid traces my brush left upon the paper . . . as delicate and transparent as a river of dreams, flowing from my fingertips and transforming everything I touched into pools of color and light and shade. With only a dab of black, something remarkable would happen on the paper: shadows slowly spread across the pastel pool, dark clouds formed on the azure horizon, and rain began to fall among the sweet peas and peacocks. Enchanted by the magic of watercolor, I sat back and smiled at my grandmother. Then my conversation with Larry darkened my thoughts, like a dab of black. I asked Grandma Amana about Jews.

"Where do they come from?" I asked.

"I think they come from the same place as all the other white people. But I've never met one of them."

"Do you think Alexander Miller is a Jew?" I asked.

"From what he says, he was born across the sea in a place called Greece. So he must be a Greek."

"Then why does he have a Jewish name?" I asked. "Why is he called Miller?"

"His name isn't Miller. It's Milas. And why should you worry about things like that?"

"Because I want to ask him if he'll give me some money for the chores I do around the house. And from what I hear, if he's a Jew he won't give me anything."

"That's a lot of nonsense," Grandma Amana exclaimed. "I don't like hearing you talk like that! Isn't it bad enough that people hate Indians?"

"Well, if his name is Milas, then why does he want

to have a Jewish name like Miller?" I insisted.

"Who knows about these crazy people in the motion-picture business? All of them change their names. They even tried to get your father to change his name when he was a stuntman. The fools didn't think 'Jamie' sounded Indian! A lot of nonsense," she huffed. "They always want to be something they aren't. If Alexander was named Miller, I bet that he would call himself Milas!"

I put my paintbrush down and nodded in confusion. "If Alexander doesn't know who he is, then how in the world can I ever figure out who I am?" I asked.

My grandmother smiled as she brushed back my unruly hair. Then she gazed intently into my eyes and said: "You will find out that who you really are is here . . . here in your pictures."

Nine

————————————

It was in the fall, when the creek widened into a river, that Reno came to live at the house of Alexander Miller.

"Now you can be with your big brother," Jemina explained. "Won't that be nice, honey?"

I remained silent and looked intently at my mother, unwilling to tell her that Reno had abandoned me long ago.

"Won't that be nice, Sy?" she insisted.

"Yes," I lied as she smoothed my hair and smiled vacantly. Then she went back to the living room where her lady friends were playing cards.

Grandma Amana took me by the shoulders and looked at me as she shook her head. "If you don't learn how to love people," she whispered, "then you will never be loved by anybody else. Whatever Reno did to you— whatever he didn't do—should not matter if you love him."

"I do love him, but he doesn't love me!" I exclaimed bitterly.

"What I see in your eyes, Sitko, is not love. It's anger."

"I hate him for not loving me," I murmured with remorse.

"If you hate him, then you also hate yourself. Why do you waste your life hating people?"

"I hate him," I repeated.

"That is only because you love him so much."

I pulled away from my grandmother and shook my head as I ran out of the kitchen. I needed to be with Larry.

I crossed the creek and cautiously peered toward his house, to be sure that his father wasn't close. When I caught sight of Larry, I waved my arms. In a few moments he snuck through the garden, hiding among the tall cornstalks, and finally joined me behind a clump of willows at the water's edge.

"Boy, is my dad sore at you," Larry whispered. "He said he's gonna go to school and tell the principal you used all kinds of dirty words."

"Pachuco is a dirty word too!"

"Sy, I don't think you should have sassed him, 'cause he's got a terrible mean temper, and he's likely to do what he's threatened and tell the principal on you. Then you'll really catch it."

"Do you really think he'll report me?"

"He's still angry . . . but he's pretty lazy too, and he's

never once gone to the school. Maybe he's just trying to scare me. He said he'd whip my bottom if I ever went off with you again."

I looked at Larry, full of anxiety for both of us. My dread must have shown, for Larry smiled and said: "But I never do nothing my pa tells me!"

"Then you and me . . . we're friends. Right?"

"Right!" Larry laughed. "The Jolly Green Giant and the Moose! Just a couple of shitkickers—that's what we are!"

And we laughed so loudly that Larry's mother came out on the back porch and looked around suspiciously.

"I better go," Larry whispered. "I'll see you tomorrow at school."

When he was safely back in his house, I went off through the tall grass with a singing heart, for I had never had a real friend before. It made me feel so good that I didn't feel like a freak anymore. *The thing about Larry and me,* I said to myself, *is that we're just different. And there's nothing wrong with that!*

It was on that morning, while I was returning home through the creek, dreaming of the day when I would be a real artist and live among people who were talented and wonderfully strange, that Reno moved into the house of Alexander Miller. When I got home, Jemina and Grandma Amana were fussing over Reno, kissing him and talking excitedly about his new home.

"Wait till you see your room, Reno! You're going to live with us at the big house! Just wait till you see it!"

my mother exclaimed with more delight than she had ever expressed toward me.

"And you come down to the little house and see my beautiful kitchen," Grandma Amana told Reno.

I turned away before they saw me, escaping to the guest house. After a while, my grandmother came in, walking slowly, a sad look on her face. She stood motionlessly by the stove, staring off into space.

"Where's Reno?" I asked softly, but she did not answer.

"Isn't he coming to see your kitchen?"

Again she did not answer.

I watched my grandmother, feeling the terrible sense of rejection and pain that was in her heart.

I went to her side. "Grandmother, are you all right?" I whispered.

She answered in a dry voice: "Reno is busy. He's too busy to come to my kitchen. He wants to stay in the big house with your mother."

After about a week, I finally approached my brother cautiously, afraid of the pain it would cause me if he turned away. Though he was exactly the same as he had been many months earlier at Star of Good Hope, somehow he seemed to be an entirely different person. Something had vanished from his eyes . . . something that I had loved in him was gone.

"How's the kid?" he said when he saw me. Then we both froze into an embarrassed silence. Finally, Reno said, "Some spread we got here, huh. Looks like we finally made it, kid."

"Made it?" I muttered, hardly able to look into his face. "Wait till you've lived here a while. This whole house is nothing but a lie. I feel more like an orphan here than I did at the Home."

"Always the dramatic one," he said with a smirk. Then, when he saw that his remark had injured me, he said: "Look, Sy, let's try to get along. Okay? Trouble with you," he said, as he lit a cigarette and gave me a disapproving look, "is you never take advantage of your opportunities. Come on, kid, for once in your life give yourself a break."

I laughed in disbelief. "Do you realize," I asked, "that I'm nobody here? I might as well be Alexander's poodle. I don't even have my own name anymore. Everything from the past is supposed to just vanish. I'm not allowed to talk about my own father," I exclaimed. "Give myself a break? I don't even know how old I am! Every six months somebody tells me it's my birthday!"

Reno shrugged and blew smoke into the air. "Well, nothing's perfect," he said.

"And it's not just me," I insisted. "They treat Grandma Amana like some sort of freak, afraid she'll embarrass them or something. She's starting to slip away from me. We don't talk much anymore. It's as if she's given up and is just waiting to die. She tells me that she doesn't know where Jamie is, but I know she sees him. What hurts is that she's afraid to tell me about it. I guess she thinks I'll tell her secret to Alexander when I'm having an argument with him."

"That's what I mean, Sy," Reno said as he put his

hand on my shoulder and shook his head with concern. "Instead of making the most of all the things Alexander is willing to give you, you keep harping about somebody like Jamie. Can't you get it into your head that our father doesn't give a damn about us? I mean, where the hell is he? What has he ever done for us? *Nothing!* That's what he's done. Can't you understand that after all this time?"

His words infuriated me. "Stop it, Reno! Stop it right now!"

Reno sighed and backed away, smiling unpleasantly. "It's a hell of a lot better to be here, Sy, than in that damn Home or out on the street. Trouble is you won't ever face facts. You've got to live in that damn dream world of yours."

I gazed intently at my brother, recalling how I had once admired his strength and popularity. Now I saw him very differently: somebody who had never grown up. My gaze must have bothered him, for he laughed defiantly and shook his head. "Okay, so we disagree. That's nothing new. But here we are, Sy, and I'm not letting anybody blow this chance for me. So let's try to get along. The name of the game is survival. The sooner you find that out, the better off you're going to be."

Now it was my turn to scoff at him. "You're still out there on the baseball field," I muttered. "Jesus, I don't believe it. The high school hero!"

"Okay, Sy, that's enough," he said in a voice full of warning. "Just don't press your luck. So what? So I was a high school hero. But this is what I decided when

Alexander asked me to come live with all of you. I decided that whatever they want me to be—that's what I'm gonna be. It's a tough world out there, Sy. Ideals won't get you very far, believe me. But if that's what you want, fine. Just leave me out of it."

Then Reno turned and walked away.

Alexander Miller grew to like Reno. He said that Reno was his kind of person. So he introduced him to his friends at the studio and at the country club. He even got him a job in the casting office, and eventually Reno earned enough money to buy a convertible. Now we didn't see very much of him. Grandma Amana and I sat silently over our dinner in her big kitchen, while Reno gave parties with Alexander and Jemina. We could hear the laughter and the voices of people talking and having a good time, echoing down the hill from the big house. I was painting while Grandma Amana washed dishes. We had not talked about Reno since the day of his arrival. Tonight, however, she put down the dishcloth and spoke resolutely, as if she had spent much time thinking about what she wanted to say.

"You can be one family," she said, "and not be of one spirit. But you must not think that you have failed, Sitko. I scolded you for thinking bad thoughts about your brother. I don't want you to become angry because the world is cruel to you. Anger is no good. It will devour your spirit. It will turn you into all the things you detest. Make your pictures and be yourself, Sitko. Don't be afraid because you are different from other people. It is your destiny to be whoever you are . . . and that is why the world is filled with wonder, because there are so many different, strange and marvelous people . . . so many unexpected things."

"But . . . I want Reno to love us . . ." I began, unable to speak as tears came into my eyes.

"No, no, no . . ." Grandma Amana murmured as we embraced one another. "They will surely break your heart with all this sadness and confusion. Do not listen to them, Sitko," she moaned, gently rocking me in her arms though I towered above her and was already a young man. "You were made of love like all the splendid creatures of the world. You were made of love. And from that love you have become someone whose hands can make a wondrous thing that is called art. So do not listen to them and do not hate them, even if they hurt you. Don't let them destroy the gift that is inside of you. They are empty people who suffer when they see that you are filled with beauty that flows from your fingertips. But do not let them break your heart, Sitko. They are to be pitied, but you must never hate them. For it is hate and envy that has robbed them of what they might have been. And it is hatred that makes them envy the miracle that you have become."

I drew away from her and went to the window. I wanted to believe her, but she was old and alien to the world. I was afraid she might be wrong. "But Grandmother," I said slowly, "I am such a stupid, ugly boy."

She started to object, but I interrupted her. "No, no . . ." I insisted, "I know it's true. And because I know

that it's true, I cannot understand how somebody like
me—somebody so plain and ignorant and clumsy—could
do *anything* that would make people envious."

My grandmother nodded. A knowing smile gradually
lighted her face.

"No," I said, "you must answer my questions if I am
to believe you. If I have so many good things inside of
me, why is it that I can't make jokes and be clever like
other people?"

"Come here . . . come here to me, Sitko," she whispered, "because I need to explain these things to you.
It is true, you are becoming a big fellow, but there are
many things you do not understand. There are some
things that only Grandma Amana can teach you. And
do you know where I keep these things? I keep them
here—in my breast. I keep them alive inside of me. Do
you understand? When you write things down, when
you make pictures of them, then you do not have to
remember them any longer. They disappear into books,
and they get lost on paper. But everything that I have
learned in my life is kept alive inside of me: our history,
our family, our wisdom. All of this is alive within me.
And as long as there are old ones to tell children these
precious things, there will never be an end to us. For
we live in our memories and in our dreams . . . we live
in our thoughts and in our visions. Do you understand,
Sitko?"

"Yes," I said. "I understand."

"It will be difficult for you, child. This I know, for I
am an old woman. It doesn't matter what happens to

me. But you matter! You matter very much to me, child. So remember to keep alive in your heart everything you have been and keep alive all that you are becoming. Do not be afraid, Sitko. Do you promise your grandmother that you will not be afraid of being yourself? Do you promise me that you will not let them make you ashamed of who you are?"

"Yes," I said with all my heart. "I promise you."

Grandma Amana smiled and wiped her nose with the back of her hand. "Then," she said happily, "I think you are ready for my final gift."

A few days later Grandma Amana gave me a bundle that was hidden away in the bottom of the string bag in which she kept all of her possessions. She also gave me a brown paper bag filled with crackers, and a bottle of water. She told me it was time for me to go to the creek where powerful beings lived, and to stay there all day and all night, and perhaps for another day and night.

"Listen to me," she murmured. "It is Saturday and the school is closed. I will tell Jemina where you have gone. And Alexander Miller and Reno will not be back until next week; so this is the time when you must go, Sitko."

"But, Grandmother . . ." I started anxiously.

"You must not ask me anything," she interrupted, putting her warm hands upon my lips. "You must do exactly as I tell you. You have matches for a fire. You have water. You must go out by yourself and wait for a vision. Do you understand?"

Before I could answer she handed me the provisions she had prepared, and then she carefully placed the hide-covered bundle inside my jacket and walked with me to the kitchen door.

"*A-koo-na-chim-moy-e-scop.* . . . Let us pray," she whispered as she touched me lightly upon the shoulder and nodded mysteriously.

"We are far from the sacred places of our grandfathers," she chanted. "We are far from the bones of our people, but perhaps there is one powerful being in the creek who will take pity upon my grandson and who will fill his life with wonderment and power. I pray to the great mystery for my grandson who cannot say the words that must be said. Give him those words! Give him a strong song to sing so his life will be good! Give him the eyes with which to see the mysteries of our people!"

Then she pressed me forward, out the kitchen door, into the yard and down into the creek where the frogs and crickets joined in my grandmother's song . . . and where the Moon came down through the evening clouds and peered into my face to see if I was the scar-faced child in whom the Morning Star lives.

It is night and it is cold. All the bark and wood I gathered is wet, and I cannot start a fire. I sit in the darkness, surrounded by noises that come from deep within the crevices of the earth and among the high, black branches. I want to find Larry's house and tap at his window so he will come out and share my ordeal, but I must remain by myself, or I will not find what I have come out into the night to discover. I sit perfectly still, trying to remember a song, trying to recall the words that Grandma Amana taught me long, long ago. When I become very tired, I stand up and raise my arms, shaking them in the cold air so I will not fall asleep. And when footsteps resound in the thickets I tell my heart to be brave. When strange sounds surround me I remind myself that all creatures are my brothers and that I belong in their world, as they belong in mine. And when all the distant lights in the houses of the San Fernando Valley go out, and the headlights of automobiles vanish from the horizon, I shiver and pray that I will not fail to open my heart to the gift that my grandmother has pleaded for me to receive from the night.

Now it is almost morning. The dew has come down upon the grass and the first birds of day are stirring and making their feeble peeping. Although I struggle to stay awake, I cannot keep my eyes open. I feel mortified that I cannot follow my grandmother's instructions, and I dig my fingernails into my palms in anger. The pain forces me to my feet. I open my heart to the morning, and I try to see the mist that is forming above the rushing, cold water of the creek. Then I sit down and fill my hands with grass, pulling it from the earth and rubbing it across my face. The smell fills my nostrils. I am overwhelmed by the sweetness of the grass, by the pungent warmth of the earth that clings to its delicate roots. Then suddenly I hear it. A small voice somewhere just in front of me in the dimness of the dawn. I strain to see, but the light is so frail that I cannot see. Gradually the Sun comes immense and glowing over the horizon and points his long golden *fingers into a clump of trees. I gasp and begin to weep, for at last I can see what I prayed to see.*

My vision came from the burned-out trunk of an ancient tree. It was a small red fox with the eyes of a woman and the genitals of a man. I could only see the animal very vaguely at first, but as the wind came up and the clouds whirled into motion, the sky filled with light, and in this storm of illumination I could see the animal very clearly. The Fox crept from the old tree and posed motionlessly for a long time, peering at me as if it knew me. I do not know why, but the sight of that powerful being made me cry out in pain. And at that very moment, the Fox dashed into the dimness, flared up momentarily, turned first into a white bird and then into a particle of light cast into the awesome emptiness of the sky.

"Hey!" I shout. "Don't leave me!"

But there is no reply. I sit down dejectedly, fearing that I have lost my one encounter with the unknown, when suddenly something touches me. I whirl around and find myself facing a pale, slender young man with bright-red hair and deep, green eyes.

"These are the things I give to you," he whispers to me without moving his lips. "These are the things," he says, tracing something in the air with a long white finger, leaving glowing lines that hang in the air like smoke. "These are for you."

When I am completely surrounded by colors, he comes very close to me and places his frosty finger upon my forehead. The imprint remains forever upon my brow.

"These colors will be your song."

And then he is gone.

Ten

━━━━━━━━━━━━

G reat yellow machines rumbled in the splendid au-
tumn grass, opening wide brown cuts in the land
and roaring as mechanical arms tossed trees and stones
into the air. The earth groaned and rolled over. Red
ants and their squirming white grubs erupted to the
surface, blinded by the sun. Horned lizards and spiders,
dragonflies and fieldmice perished under grinding metal
feet. And soon the familiar landscape of my childhood
vanished, leaving a terrible silence and countless rows
of ugly little houses and flowers held prisoner by picket
fences.

Plastic flamingos walked arrogantly across carefully
manicured lawns, while electric toasters and Mixmasters
hummed in chorus with washing machines and vacuum
cleaners. Shopping carts rolled relentlessly through
immense refrigerated markets. And I watched in astonishment as crowds of jelly-filled people with powdered-
sugar smiles surrounded the great house of Alexander

Milas-Miller, turning the San Fernando Valley into a vast sea of small dreams and aspirations.

The new people sent their children to our little school, where they easily swept past Larry and me, taking places at the head of the class. The children of the movie families began to vanish into private schools, but Larry and I had no place to hide from the ceaseless deluge of candy-coated kids. We sank deeper into ourselves as they pushed us ever backward into a place where we became invisible. To Larry, it didn't matter, but I was beginning to feel a powerful resentment for my situation. I could see Larry vanishing under the asphalt like the red ants and the lizards, while I struggled against annihilation by swearing and fighting and being unrestrainedly stupid and cruel.

"Who the hell do you think you are!" I shouted at a couple of girls as they hurried down the school hallway, ignoring me. "You stuck-up bitch!"

I rushed after them, hurling insults. I shouted and laughed at them, saying anything that came to mind. Students looked at me with anger and disapproval, but I didn't care any longer. If they didn't like me, at least they couldn't ignore me.

"What the hell you staring at, you brownnose idiot!" I yelled.

Then, suddenly, a door opened and Mrs. Blake, my social studies teacher, confronted me.

"Come in here," she said. "I want to talk to you."

I attempted to dodge past her, but she quickly drew her silver whistle to her lips. I knew that if she blew it

I was in trouble, so I leaned with resignation against the locker-lined wall and stared at her resentfully.

"Come inside. . . . Sit down at that desk and try to get hold of yourself," she said in a voice that was neither angry nor threatening.

As I obeyed her instructions, she quietly went about her business: erasing the lesson from the blackboard, closing papers into her desk and placing a stack of blue workbooks in her battered briefcase. Then she sat down and faced me without speaking.

She was a peculiar old lady: short and square and ugly. Her face had been badly beaten by time—it had wrinkles, veins, brown splotches, and tiny white whiskers. Yet it was a gentle face, with very deep-set eyes that looked out at me through remarkably thick glasses.

I had never noticed the peacefulness of her voice.

"I understand that you paint," she said with such unexpected sympathy that I was completely caught off guard, without a nasty remark ready to throw back at her.

"I'm told," she said, "that you are quite a good artist."

I was silent, watching her carefully.

"Do you want to be an artist? Have you ever thought of studying art? Would you like to show me some of your work?"

I laughed suspiciously and made a sour face to mock her, but she took no notice of my hostility.

"We have a club. We meet on the front lawn at lunchtime every Wednesday. If you would like to come, just give the gate monitor this note," she said, scribbling something on a piece of yellow paper. "We have some good artists here at school . . . and a few students who write stories and poetry too. Maybe you would like it."

I continued to look at her with an expression of resentment and mockery, but she smiled, and her face flooded with a warmth so intense that it seemed to well up from some mysterious place inside of her. I did not respond, as I snatched the note from her fingers and backed away, frightened by her kindness, intrigued by her candor, and wanting to be nice to her though I did not know how to do it.

"You've gotta come with me," I told Larry.

"Why the hell should I come to some dumb art club?" he said. "You're the artist, Sy. . . . I'm not!"

"Listen to me, Larry," I implored. "You gotta come. Just do me a favor and come to one meeting. You don't have to do anything or say anything. I just want you to come with me. Okay?"

"You're too chickenshit to go by yourself!" he muttered.

"So what! So what!"

"So plenty," he said. "You want to hang around these turkeys, but you're scared silly. So you gotta drag me into it. That's what's wrong with it! What's the matter, Sy . . . aren't we good enough without those freaks?"

The word "freaks" stung, and for a moment I intensely disliked Larry. He saw the hurt in my face, and he sighed and shrugged apologetically.

"I guess we're all freaks in one way or another," I muttered.

"Okay . . . okay . . . so what do you want me to do?" he asked.

"You don't have to say anything or do anything. I'm just asking you to come to the meeting with me."

"Jesus!" Larry pouted as he blew hard between his lips and paced back and forth with indecision. "And then what?" he asked.

"Then . . ." I stammered, "then nothing. I want to see what these guys are up to. And I don't want to go by myself. I thought about it a lot, and I decided that I want to go . . . but I can't go alone. So do me this favor and come along with me just for the heck of it. Okay?"

"Okay."

"What a bunch of clods!" Larry whispered as we sat on the lawn eating, surrounded by the eight members of the Art Club. "I don't believe these guys!"

I nodded in agreement with my friend, although I was actually fascinated by this peculiar assembly of misfits. I had seen most of them in class or in the halls, but now it was as if I were seeing them for the first time.

Joanne Beale had always struck me as a silent and weird girl—tough-mannered, tall and plain, with a transparent mustache, which she covered with her index finger whenever she was called upon to answer questions in class. But at the Art Club meeting she unfolded like a holiday tablecloth, revealing an unexpected beauty and complexity—fresh and fragile and strong.

John Smith and Tom Todd were called sissies. I had avoided them, because everyone howled with abuse if someone talked to them. It was terrifying the way John and Tom were treated. I had often been ignored and ridiculed, but there was no ridicule as horrible as that which John and Tom faced every day at school. The very thought of such treatment was unbearable to me. But even at the Art Club meeting, I hesitated to display my admiration for the delicate and beautiful woodcarvings of animals John had made.

"Je-sus!" Larry muttered under his breath as John lovingly unwrapped his carvings with long, graceful fingers which did not seem to belong to a boy. "Je-sus," Larry repeated when John began to speak about his artwork in a peculiarly soft and lilting voice.

I was overwhelmed by confusion, for I felt obliged to join Larry in his contempt for these outcasts; but at the same time I felt admiration and respect for their talent. I glanced hesitantly at John Smith as he spoke about his love of animals.

His soft face and piercing eyes confused and frightened me. I was appalled by the strange gentleness of his voice and the extravagance of his movements. And yet I was fascinated by the wonderful objects he had carved. I could not reconcile my scorn with my admiration.

For as long as I could remember, the students had called Tom Todd by the name *Tom Toad*. I had done it too, trying to join the others, because it made me feel less of an outsider. Now, as Tom read his poems aloud, I was ashamed of myself.

Tom was more disliked than anyone at school. The mention of "Tom Toad" made everyone laugh. I don't think any of us really understood why we mocked Tom; we just did it. He was blind in one eye, and his hands were horribly deformed—gnarled and misshapen, with only three fingers on one hand and four on the other. We made fun of him, chanting insults when he passed, and giggling when he spoke in class. Even the most disliked and ignored of us were momentarily accepted by the most popular students whenever we joined one another in our cruel treatment of Tom Todd. His deformity made us feel important and superior. And yet now, as I listened to the marvelous words he had written, I discovered the person who had to live inside Tom's grotesque body.

The student who most fascinated me at the Art Club meeting was Susan Summer. She had never been one of the misfits. Fiercely good-looking, with a strongly sculptured face and dazzling, shiny black hair, she was so confident and articulate that I sat in awe of her as she spoke her thoughts and expressed her ideas. She seemed much older than the rest of us. Nothing intimidated Susan. She had an opinion about everything. She intrigued and frightened me to such an extent that I could not speak to her or look at her.

"And what about you . . ." she said, looking over at me with such an open and candid expression that it seemed as if we were old friends, "what do you do?"

Larry groaned and slouched deep into his lumber jacket.

For a moment I was unable to answer, fearful of Larry's disapproval and intimidated by Susan Summer's blunt manner. But I was determined to follow the example of the others, who had talked freely about themselves and their art.

"I draw. . . . I paint. . . . I make pictures," I said with effort.

"Maybe next time Seymour will bring some of his work and talk to us about it," Mrs. Blake interjected, as if she understood my embarrassment.

"Next time. . . ." Larry mumbled from within his big coat. "Fat chance!"

I laughed automatically and then felt like a fool, as I realized no one else had found Larry amusing.

Susan Summer looked at me, her large black eyes pinning me to the grass like a butterfly in a cardboard sample box. I could feel her taking me apart, piece by piece. I turned away, suffocating under her scrutiny. But I had to glance back at her as she talked. Whatever Susan Summer said intrigued me not so much for its meaning as for the utter conviction with which she spoke.

On that day, as I sat on the lawn next to Larry, I began to suspect that I wanted from people something that my good friend could not give to me. On that afternoon, a door gradually opened, and it was only with its opening that I could hear the frantic knocking that had long resounded within me. And as the members of the Art Club read their stories and recited their poems, as they displayed their drawings and carvings, I felt an enormous kinship to them. I looked into their eyes and I saw myself—my shyness and self-consciousness, my fear of

disapproval and my contempt for authority and medi-
ocrity. I gazed at them in recognition and admiration,
but at the same time, I felt that I was somehow betraying
my friendship with Larry.

Eleven

_____

Dinner was the worst time at the big house of Alexander Milas-Miller. After school I could escape from the arguments and anguish of Jemina and Alexander. I could sit quietly with my grandmother as she dozed. I could look at the pictures in the art books Mrs. Blake checked out of the library for me. Or I could paint. And when my fingers failed me and no images rose to the surface of my mind, I went to the creek, barking three times from behind the willows near Larry's home. Then the two of us would silently roam the land or walk along the newly paved streets, lined with countless unoccupied tract houses, with blank windows and naked, treeless yards. Sometimes Larry would talk his mother into letting him have the keys to their old pickup truck, and we took turns roaring up and down back roads where cows and palominos scattered before the noise of the motor.

But at dinnertime, I had to go back to the house of Alexander Miller. Grandma Amana and I no longer enjoyed the seclusion of meals at the guest house. Jemina had decided that all of us should have dinner together. Each evening we assembled at the big house and sat around the large table in the dining room.

When Alexander came home from the motion-picture studio he sat in a terrible gloom. He banged his fist on the table so the dishes rattled and my stomach turned sour. Or he lapsed into a silence full of impending violence. Or he shouted at Jemina and me. But he never shouted at Reno.

Grandma Amana moved slowly around the table, serving each of us while Alexander shouted. She did not seem to hear him or see him.

"I'll tell you one thing," Alexander shouted. "I don't want him moping around the house, making those damn pictures all day! I want him outside doing something for his keep. There's lots of work around here! And I'm not spending my money on gardeners when he's able to do the job. So you just tell that damn son of yours that he'd better start doing something for his keep or I'll throw him the hell out of here!" he yelled as he thumped on the table with his fist. "He wouldn't be some kind of half-wit if he was my son! I'd kick the daylights out of him before I'd have my son acting like some kind of pansy—with those damn paints and pictures and books!"

I watched Alexander Miller with dread. When he wasn't criticizing me, he would begin on my mother— her extravagance, her lies, her debt to him for taking care of her children and her mother. And then he would begin to drink with my brother, and slowly his lips loos-

ened and his empty blue eyes filled with goldfish and
bubbles, and he would whimper and weep about his
dead father and the lost virtue of his sister and the
ingratitude of my father who had run off to freedom
and deserted us. Late at night, when my brother had
passed out on the floor and Alexander Miller sat in his
big leather chair, rocking back and forth as he hummed
some old song and wept, Grandma Amana and I finished
washing and drying the dishes and slipped away before
he began shouting again.

Even from the guest house I could hear Jemina and
Alexander arguing as I gazed at my pictures that covered
the walls of my bedroom. In the morning I could still
hear them shouting at one another. The only place where
it was peaceful was in the kitchen of Grandma Amana.

"Don't worry about them," she told me with sorrow
filling her old face. "Your mother loves you . . . but she
does not know how to make you feel loved."

"She knows how to make Reno feel loved," I thought.

I kissed my grandmother on the forehead, and she
looked up at me helplessly. "I am too old, Sitko," she
whispered. "I am too old. I want to help you, but I no
longer have the strength . . ." she murmured. "If only
your father would come back to us. I have prayed so
often for Jamie Ghost Horse to come back . . . but he
must be very far away because he never hears my pray-
ers."

Then she sighed and folded her hands in her lap. "Do
you think your father will ever come back to us?" she
droned, peering out into the night as if she expected

the answer from something distant and mysterious.

I embraced her gently, overcome by the fragility of her tiny body, by the helplessness of her twisted fingers and the frail light that still glowed in her ancient eyes. Those eyes, full of strength and fear and death, haunted me. When I looked into them I plummeted into time—falling endlessly through every day that had ever existed. In my grandmother's eyes there were three hundred sunrises and ten thousand moonless nights. In her eyes were the beginning of the world and the last golden light of the final Sun.

"You are a good boy," she whispered.

As I embraced her again, I could feel her bones pressing through her emaciated flesh. And in the long folds of her throat I could see her pulse tugging desperately at life, fighting to keep her body alive.

". . . a good boy."

I began to chant a song of the Fox until, at last, she fell asleep.

I was no longer a boy. When I looked into the mirror I saw a tall, slender figure with a child's hands and a grief-stricken face. Now when I was alone my fingers released a downpour of rain and a blizzard of lightning and hail. Color and sparks ignited my fingertips, and pictures gushed from them. Slowly I found my way back into the north country upon a white and purple highway that flowed through my mind. Now my paintings filled me with an entirely new person I had never been before. Slowly I walked into the solitude of myself and I closed the door behind me, shutting away everything that was painful and ugly. And for a time I was safe.

One afternoon Larry shouted to me from across the bridge. His mother had been sick.

"It's pretty bad," he told me in a weak voice, "and it looks like my mother's never coming home again. Pa says she's really gone for good."

I touched my friend's hand and shook my head, not knowing what to do to ease the terrible pain I saw in his eyes.

"Anyway . . . I had to stay home to look after things while my pa stayed with my mother at the hospital," Larry was saying as we tramped through the foxtails toward the vegetable garden near his house. "My pa says we don't even have enough money for a decent burial. Pa says it's bad times for us now that the doctors took all our money."

I reached into my pocket for the money I had been saving to repay Larry's loan. I held it out to him, but Larry slowly shook his head.

"Naw, you keep it, Sy . . . 'cause it's a present from me to you," he stammered as we neared the shed where Larry's father often worked. I peered cautiously in that direction, fearing that we would get in trouble. But Larry didn't seem to be worried about his father. Soon I understood why. He didn't take any notice of us as we walked to the back door of Larry's house. He sat listlessly on an apple crate, his gray eyes staring off and his hard, narrow mouth hung with remorse. He wasn't angry anymore.

"So," Larry whispered as we walked past his forlorn father, ". . . it's something like a going-away present from me to you, Sy. 'Cause Pa says we're selling out to them Jews after all, and we'll be leaving here for good and always."

Then my friend covered his face and turned away from me in shame as he wept.

I left him standing beside his father, and walked in circles through the pools of watercress until the water soaked into my boots, and all the light vanished from the sky.

Twelve

There are other worlds.

This is what I learned from the lessons of my fingers. In my pictures there was a day that had not yet dawned upon the world, and there was a peaceful place for me among the streets and meadows that I spread with thick, rich colors across sheets of paper. It was not my world, but an ancient and sacred place that I had merely dreamed back into existence with my fingers, with my art. When I awakened into that world I found myself among people from whom I gradually learned a remarkable language of images and ideas—a secret language which mystified and often angered people like Alexander Miller who were forever closed off in a world without art.

Alexander became more abusive as I learned that language. Now I cared nothing for his approval. He was no longer capable of making me doubt my talent or my worth. One day at lunchtime, Susan Summer said, "The only reason he detests your pictures is because they are from an incomprehensible world he can never enter."

Her extravagant language pleased me, and I laughed.

"You must take the upper hand," she said with a victorious gesture. "When people give me a hard time, I don't worry about it. I just say: 'You can't reject me, because I banished you!' "

I began to wrestle with difficult ideas. I badgered myself until I was no longer afraid of books. And I began to read with a passion. *Proust, Kafka, Faulkner, Joyce, Woolf, Eliot, Mann, Gide* . . . names that became magical to me! Then I discovered music. Susan was an usher for a concert series, and just before performances began, she let me slip into the auditorium and find an unoccupied chair. Suddenly the music of Arnold Schönberg and Anton Webern soared in my head, making me rethink everything I had ever felt about art. And when we were on the bus back to the Valley, Susan and I argued about the concert and the books we were reading, the exhibitions we had seen, and everything else. Susan Summer never stopped talking. She used her intellect like a weapon. She was a lancer, thrashing with remarkable precision at the world she disdained . . . always aiming for the heart. She would settle for nothing less than a kill. And I always died gracefully at the end of our debates, because I liked her and also because she was much more clever than I.

Susan was an organizer. She was always talking us into some kind of exceptional project. The year before she graduated and disappeared from my life, she told the members of the Art Club that it was time for us to produce our own magazine. And so all of us spent every lunchtime in Mrs. Blake's room, typing stories and poems on stencils, making woodblocks for illustrations, and mimeographing, sorting and stapling fifty copies of our magazine. When it was finished Tom Todd picked up a copy in his twisted hands and smiled shyly as he awkwardly turned to the pages where his poems were printed.

All of us were very proud of the magazine. Joanne Beale had made the woodcut for the cover, and there were four of my drawings among the stories that Susan Summer had written. I recall that afternoon when the project was finally done, and we sat down in exhaustion—the stacks of blue booklets piled around us. Mrs. Blake poured punch, and John Smith cut the cake he had made for us. We all talked at once and laughed, until suddenly we fell silent and looked at one another with immense admiration and affection.

I was not surprised when a monitor came into Mrs. Blake's room and told me that the school principal wanted to see me in his office. I was always in some kind of trouble during these days of self-discovery, and I had already accepted the fact that nothing I did was ever equal to what was expected of me.

"Your father came to see me," the principal said. "He tells me that you're in a shell. Do you know what that means, Seymour? He says that you don't have any friends, and that you work too hard at your studies and spend all the rest of your time making pictures."

I did not respond.

"I know that art is very important to you. And that's

all very nice. But, you know, Seymour, there are other things in life besides pictures and books. You need to be a well-rounded fellow if you want to be successful. Your adviser tells me that you never attend school dances. And the coach says that you constantly skip your physical education class. I don't think I've ever seen you at a football game. . . ." The principal paused and looked at me for a long time as if he gradually realized that I was mocking him with my silence. Then he sighed with impatience and added, "Do you understand what I'm talking about, Seymour? And if you do, why can't you speak up like a man?"

I did not want to look at him for fear that he would recognize the contempt in my eyes.

"Do you hear what I'm saying to you!" he exclaimed with growing anger.

"Yes, I understand!" I muttered, unable to restrain myself any longer. "Yes, I understand *exactly* what you are saying! But the problem is that you don't know what you're talking about! For one thing, Alexander Miller is not my father. And he's not married to my mother. If you really want to know the truth: he sleeps with my mother but he's not my mother's husband. He is not a nice man, and I don't give a damn what he thinks about me! What I do with my free time is none of his business, and it's also none of your business." Then I glared at him as my rage overflowed. "You can't punish me because I paint pictures! And you can't punish me for not going to football games!"

The principal grabbed me and began to slap me violently. I was nearly the man's height but I silently submitted to him. When I didn't back away, his rage flared and he beat me with his fists. Each time he struck me I saw in flashes the headmaster of Star of Good Hope, and I saw the tattered Chinese garden, and I saw the jeering faces of classmates. I also saw the expression of satisfaction that filled the principal's face as he hit me. But I no longer felt pain, so great was the rage that filled me. I added each blow to all the other blows of my life, I added the pain to all the rest of the pain. When blood began to flow from my nose, the principal pushed me away and fell into his chair, staring at my battered face as if he did not believe what he had done to me. I wiped the blood away with my sleeve. I stared at him. Then I walked out of his office and slammed the door.

I grappled in the darkness until I touched my sketchbook, and then without opening my eyes I scribbled until I had made an image of the principal's face. All the lines collided over him, so he lay dead beneath the sharp point of my pencil.

When I finally got out of bed to go up to the big house for dinner, the pain still lingered in my cheeks. Reno looked into my room on his way home from work. He glanced at my open sketchbook and said, "Y'know, the reason nobody will ever buy anything you draw is 'cause none of it ever looks like anything recognizable."

When I didn't respond he added, "That's what comes from reading too much."

"Do me a favor, will you, Reno, and get the hell out of here," I muttered, looking up for the first time. He stared at my bruised face.

"Jesus, Seymour, sometimes I don't believe you," he exclaimed when he realized I had been punished again. "You're not going to live through high school if this keeps up! They don't have the right to beat the hell out of you all the time!"

For a moment my brother gazed at me with an expression of concern I had not seen in his face for a very long time. Then he murmured, "You okay, Sitko?"

I smiled at him and shook my head with the pleasure of hearing him say my real name. "Yeah," I said with a surge of affection, "I'll be fine."

"You sure?"

"I'm sure. I'll see you up at the house in a few minutes. Okay?"

He continued to look at me with concern and then he awkwardly embraced me and left the room.

At dinner Jemina sat silently while Grandma Amana cleared away the dishes and touched me gently on the shoulder as she passed me.

Alexander always objected to any show of feeling between my grandmother and me, and so he began complaining to show his annoyance.

"Look at him, will you," he said. "He looks like some kind of beatnik or something! I'm ashamed to have people know he's my son!"

"*Au-wah-tsahps*. . . . Screwball," Grandma Amana whispered with a grin as she leaned over to take my plate.

"And I thought I told your mother to stop talking like that!"

"Mother . . . please stop annoying him," Jemina pleaded. "The two of you just can't be happy unless you're making trouble."

Alexander pounded his fist on the table and leaped to his feet so that his chair crashed to the floor. I watched him as he ranted—his throat bulging with profanities and his immense belly heaving to and fro as he strutted around the dinner table. I knew he hated my silence. He detested what I might be thinking. He worked himself into a terrible rage, hoping to frighten me. But I had learned to defy him despite the panic inside of me. I would not show him what I felt.

Finally he retreated from the dining room, leaving my mother trembling and my grandmother groaning as she carried the dishes into the kitchen. Reno was already drunk and had passed out in his chair.

Jemina drew a breath and gazed at me as if she could not understand me. "You're a troublemaker," she said. "You must get some kind of satisfaction in making me miserable. Is that what you're trying to do, Seymour?"

Grandma Amana gestured for me to be silent. I picked up my sketchbook and started for the door.

"Seymour!" my mother shouted. "I didn't say you were excused!"

I turned without expression and faced her.

"Oh, what's the use," she murmured. "Do what you want to do. It doesn't matter."

"May I be excused?" I asked sarcastically.

My mother ignored my tone, but tears came into her eyes. I suddenly felt dreadful for hurting her. "I'm sorry," I whispered.

"It doesn't matter," she said, blowing her nose on a tiny handkerchief and smiling with effort. Then she abruptly changed the subject. "On Saturday there's going to be a party for some nice young people at Maxine Brown's house, and I asked her mother to invite you, Seymour. I bought you a lovely new shirt and you can wear the blue sweater that's too small for Reno."

I looked at my mother in astonishment. "But Mother . . ." I protested.

"Please, Seymour—no more arguments tonight. I don't ask many things of you. But this is very important to me. So please tell me that you'll accept the invitation . . . for my sake."

Again my grandmother gestured to me, and after a moment I shook my head in resignation. "Okay . . . if it means that much to you, I'll go."

Maxine Brown was a fat girl with a large nose and watery eyes. Her father was an agent for actors and her mother was one of those blond ladies with little black eyebrows drawn over her colorless eyes. The Brown family lived in a big house on Laurel Canyon. It was a fantastic building, with weathercocks on the turrets and a tall entrance gate leading to a huge front door. When

I rang the bell I heard a whole chorus of chimes, and then a black woman in a uniform came to the door and asked for my name.

When I explained that I had come for the party, she looked me up and down and stepped aside so I could enter. The living room was filled with parents. Their glances made me nervous. The maid wanted to take my lumber jacket, but I didn't want everyone to see that the lining was torn, so I carried it with me as I made my way toward the pool patio where the young people were dancing.

Mrs. Brown spotted me and brought her daughter, Maxine, to greet me. "Well," she said, "there you are, Seymour. We didn't think you were going to make it. Your mother told me that you absolutely detest parties. Well, we'll have to do something about that, won't we? So come along, dear, and get some punch, and Maxine will introduce you to all these nice people your mother is so terribly anxious for you to meet. Come along, dear, don't be bashful, for goodness' sake . . . and why don't you get rid of that perfectly awful jacket so you can relax."

Maxine grudgingly nodded to me as her mother left us. She took me by the hand and led me in a circle around the pool, introducing me to the same people that I saw every day in school. Most of them didn't turn to look at me. A few of the girls nodded and looked away, and the guys glanced at me with contempt. Maxine gave me a cup of punch, and then I was left alone.

"Seymour Miller," Mrs. Brown called out to me, when she saw that I was standing by myself, "don't mope around, dear. Go ask one of the girls for a dance."

"Thank you, Mrs. Brown," I said. "I'm not much good at dancing."

She looked at me with dismay, and then she said, "Well, be a good fellow and take this punch bowl into the kitchen and get it refilled."

When I found the kitchen it was crowded with servants. I put the punch bowl on the sink and tried to get someone's attention, but they passed me by as they rushed about their business. I shrugged and started to make my retreat through the back door, when I heard someone calling me.

"*Pssst!* You . . . yes, you. Come over here."

It was an old woman in a long skirt and an apron. She had her hair tied back, and her face was so full of pouches and wrinkles that she looked almost as old as Grandma Amana.

"*Pssst!* I'm talking to you. Come over here. I want you to tell me your name," she insisted.

"Seymour Miller," I said.

She looked at me dubiously and then gestured for me to follow her. She limped down the hall and into a tiny sitting room filled with faded photographs and old furniture. I decided that she must be the housekeeper.

She lowered herself slowly into a large armchair, and beckoned for me to sit in front of her. I hesitated. I wanted to leave but didn't want to offend her.

"Don't be so shy," she said in a gentle voice. "Sit down for a little while and we can have a nice talk," she said in her odd accent.

"Yes, ma'am."

I sat on a stool in front of her.

She looked at me in the curious way that the elders look at people . . . as though they see through them. Then she nodded as if she had come to some kind of conclusion about me. As I sat under her intense gaze I was far more comfortable than I had felt among the guests.

"Here," she said, reaching into her apron and handing me a quarter. "That's a quarter for your thoughts."

I laughed and she nodded gravely. And then a little sparkle came into her eyes.

"I'm an old lady and I know things without anybody telling me. . . . I know things just from watching you. That's right, I was watching you for maybe twenty minutes. I got eyes in my head, and believe me, I know a sad fella when I see one."

I didn't respond, but it seemed to make no difference to the woman.

"How old are you?" she asked abruptly.

"I'm fourteen."

"You don't sound like you're very sure of that," she said.

"I'm not sure."

"Okay . . . so you're maybe thirteen, fourteen, fifteen. . . . My goodness, such a big fella too. Such a nice-looking young fella and yet he doesn't dance with anybody or talk to anybody." Then she smiled kindly and nodded gravely once again. "You want to be an old person like me? . . . sitting here night after night and watching other people having a good time? Is that what you want out of life? To watch?"

Something about this old woman filled me with sadness. I could not respond to her question, and I could not escape her intense gaze.

"Don't be so unhappy, Seymour Miller. . . . I'm just an old lady, and I'd like to talk to you. So don't be so uncomfortable."

Again she was silent.

"Where do you come from?" she asked. "Not around here, I betcha."

"No, ma'am. I think I come from Canada. My grandmother tells me that's where I was born."

"Ahuh . . . that's what she tells you . . . that you come from Canada. And of course you don't know. That's very interesting. Tell me, young fella, what are you doing here?"

"My . . . my father . . . works in the movies," I stammered.

"What I'm asking," she repeated gently, "is what you are doing at this party?"

I didn't know what to answer.

"Are you a friend of my granddaughter, Maxine? Do you know her at school?"

"Not really."

"Uh-huh . . ." she murmured with a nod. "And what kind of name is Seymour Miller?" she asked, looking intently into my eyes. "What kind of a name is that?"

"I think it's Jewish," I said.

"Uh-huh, so it's a Jewish name. . . ." she said with a bobbing movement of her head.

"Yes, ma'am."

"So if it's a Jewish name then that must mean that you are Jewish."

"Yes, ma'am. . . . I think so, ma'am."

"And tell me something, Seymour Miller, why is it that you want to be a Jew?"

I was silent.

"It's very funny, you know, that a boy like you should want so much to be a Jew when all my grandchildren don't want anybody to know they're Jewish. That is something I find funny in a sad kind of way, Seymour Miller." And again she bobbed her head to and fro with a deep sigh. "What a mix-up . . . what a mixed-up world this is we have here. What a mix-up," she murmured sadly. "You want to be Seymour Miller and in this house they want to be *Brown*! You don't think that's funny, but it is funny and I'll tell you why. For generations we were called Bronzinsky, but for America we've got to be *Brown*! Bronzinsky isn't good enough for America." She sighed.

"Excuse me, ma'—" I started to say.

"Don't be in such a hurry, young fella. You got your whole life in front of you . . . so you can sit here like a nice boy for a few more minutes. I have something to tell you and then you can run off and pretend to be whoever you want."

I didn't want to offend an elder who reminded me of Grandma Amana, so I reluctantly sat back down and waited.

"I'm just an old bubba. I was born in Russia so long ago that I can't remember the house I lived in when I was a child. Now we have a lot of money, but I'm still an old Jew who was born in Russia and nothing in the whole world is going to change that fact. Do you understand what I'm saying to you, Seymour Miller?"

I nodded uncomfortably, not knowing what she meant.

"You're a nice young man. Try not to be angry with me because I'm telling you the truth. I don't mean to hurt your feelings, but I want you to understand something. I don't know who you are or where you come from, but you had better try to find out who you really are, because otherwise you'll end up not being anybody at all. You got somewhere an old grandmother like me who loves you, yes? Well, make her proud of you, Seymour Miller. Don't break her heart by denying her. Do you understand what I'm trying to tell you? Don't be ashamed of her because she has a funny way of talking and a funny way of dressing. Don't break her heart," she murmured, as if she were talking to herself.

I was stung to the heart by her eyes. I leaped to my feet and ran out the back door. With outstretched arms I began to cry again and again, *"E-spoom-mo-git! . . .* Help me!"

The cry grew louder as I ran. It was so massive a cry that I could no longer contain it. Pain welled up in my throat and turned into a shout.

That old woman had stripped me naked. She had seen the desperation and confusion I hid from people. I believed I was independent and free; I claimed that I didn't care if people accepted me; I believed I was smarter and better than any of them . . . and yet I could never escape the profound longing to be loved. And this realization howled out of me as I ran down the street, turning into a scream. It was no longer my voice, but the voice of a whole race of people, screaming out of me like a terrible unrelenting plea.

Thirteen

━ ━ ━ ━ ━ ━ ━ ━

I needed to talk to Reno, but the big house was dark. His car was not in the garage, so I knew that he was out drinking.

Jemina had gone upstairs for the night. And Alexander Miller sat silently in his big chair in the den, his arms crossed over his belly as he stared off into space. I peered at him in silence, hoping that he would not notice me.

Once he had been an aerialist. I had seen the photographs in the albums in the attic. Once he had worn white tights and a sequined bolero. And Alexander Milas and Jamie Ghost Horse had flown through the air together like marvelous, glittering birds. But the circus and my father were gone. And Alexander Miller was no longer built for the air. Now his face was puffy, and the handsome young man in the faded photographs had vanished under wrinkles and fat. He no longer had a bushy mustache, and his hair was falling out, leaving a nakedness to his face that made him look like a strange, overgrown infant. Now he sat silently in his big chair. Night after night he dozed in his chair, watching something I could not see. And then he fell asleep, and a trace of saliva slowly oozed down his chin.

I backed away quickly and went to Reno's room to wait for him. I was determined to sit up until he came home, but I was so depressed and exhausted that I eventually climbed into his bed without getting undressed. I put a pillow over my head because I was afraid that at any moment I would go mad and begin to scream again. At last I fell asleep. But I could not escape myself even in my dreams. I heard Jemina and Alexander Miller yelling at one another, and I saw myself running to the closet where the rifle was kept. I rushed into the living room just as Alexander was strangling my mother. I shouted as I pointed the rifle at his head. Then I fired. The blood spouted upward in a crimson storm, blinding me . . . drenching my groin. Then the world vanished, leaving me without fingers, without eyes or visions.

When I awoke I found Reno sitting on the edge of the bed, smiling down at me.

He was drunk.

"You were having a nightmare," he stammered as he stroked my head. "You're still a little kid like you were a long time ago . . . still afraid of the dark."

I groaned and pulled the covers over my head.

"Still afraid of the bogeyman," Reno giggled as he playfully jabbed at me.

"Come on, Reno, lay off. I want to talk to you, and you're drunk again!" I implored.

"What's that supposed to mean?" he growled defensively. "What kind of a lousy remark is that supposed to be? Here I'm trying to be nice to you 'cause you were yelling bloody murder in your sleep and a lot of thanks I get for it!"

"Reno," I whispered, putting my fingers to his lips, "have a heart. The old man is just looking for an excuse to have a fight. Be quiet and listen to what I have to say. I have to get out of this house before I go crazy, Reno, and I need your help."

"No . . . no . . . no," he said with drunken concern. "I gotta talk to you, kid, 'cause that's a dumb idea. I'm the one that's got to get out of here. But you . . . you got talent, and so you got to finish school so you can make something of yourself," he stammered, fishing for something in his pockets that he couldn't find.

"I've had a terrible night," I said, realizing that he was in no condition to help me decide what to do. "And it's late. So maybe we'll wait until tomorrow and talk about it."

"I want to talk to you *now*, Sy!" he loudly exclaimed.

"Okay . . . okay . . . but not so loud."

Then his shoulders slouched and he shook his head wearily as he suddenly began to weep. "Goddamn it," he sobbed, "this life is no good. I'm ready to quit. That's how bad it is."

His sorrow was completely unexpected. I sat up in

bed and looked at my brother helplessly, realizing that all this time, while I thought he was the family favorite, he had been miserable.

"Jesus," he wept. "Our lousy father is somewhere out there . . . who knows where! Grandma Amana is half crazy! Our mother's whoring it up with that Greek bastard, and you're some kind of a nut. And look at me— I'm a goddamn alcoholic! Jesus, what a mess!"

"Come on, Reno," I murmured as I embraced him. "We can't all fall apart. Pull yourself together."

"I don't even know what the hell I'm talking about, and tomorrow I'll go back to the studio and deny every word I've said. But right now . . . right now it hurts something awful. And you're the only one who understands what I'm talking about," he sobbed.

"It's going to be okay," I lied, feeling wave upon wave of depression and desperation rolling over the great house of Alexander Miller. "I'll help you get into bed and then tomorrow when we feel better we'll talk about it. Okay?"

"No," he pleaded, clinging to my arm. "Don't go. Stay here for a while. I need you to stay here with me for a little while or I don't think I can make it. I tell you, I'm not gonna make it, Sitko," he panted as he stretched out next to me and closed his eyes.

We lay there in the darkness for a long time. Then I felt my brother's body trembling as he began to weep again.

"Jesus, Reno, what's the matter?" I whispered. "What's happening to you?"

"I'm never gonna amount to anything," he sobbed. "I'm just a fake. I don't even have any talent. Christ, what a mess I've made of things!"

"Come on," I murmured, putting my arms around him, "it's not all that bad. You're plenty smart. And you've got a good job, and you've got looks and personality. Hell, Reno, everybody always likes you."

The more I said the more he wept.

"It's all fake," he sobbed. "It's just a pile of lies."

I embraced my brother and tried to comfort him. His sobs thundered through me as he buried his face against my chest.

Then suddenly the door to the bedroom flew open and the lights went on, blinding me. I sat up in terror, not knowing what was happening.

Alexander Miller stood in the doorway shaking with rage.

"What the hell is going on in here!" he shouted. "My God, what has been going on in this house!"

I stumbled out of bed and tried to pull Reno to his feet. He was half conscious, and even Alexander's outburst did not rouse him.

"I want both of you out of this house!" Alexander was shouting again and again. "I want you perverted bastards out of my house tonight!"

"He's drunk," I exclaimed, dragging my brother out of Alexander's frenzied reach. "What's the matter with you! He's just drunk!"

"What were you two doing in here this time of night? What were you dirty Indian bastards doing in here?"

Alexander shouted as Jemina rushed into the bedroom and tried to calm him. "I'll kill both of you! I'll put a bullet in both of your perverted heads!" he roared as he snatched at us and Jemina tried to restrain him.

"Please!" Jemina cried as she held him back. "They're brothers, for god's sake! What are you thinking! They're just brothers!"

"I want both of them out of here!" Alexander said again and again, panting and straining against Jemina's grasp. "I want both of them out of this house right now!"

"Please listen to me," Jemina pleaded.

"No! No more listening to you! I want your lousy sons out of here!" Alexander bellowed, as he tore himself free and started for the hallway. "If they're still here when I get back, I'm going to blow their goddamn brains out!"

Jemina was frantic with fear. She pushed me aside and ran to Reno who was passed out on his bed. "You've got to get out of here before he kills somebody!" she cried. "Sitko," she wailed, "you're so young—he'll forgive you! But you have to help me get your brother out of here!"

While my mother pressed me forward and wept, I slapped and shook Reno until he awoke, and then Jemina and I dragged him downstairs and into the kitchen. All the while, we could hear Alexander Miller frantically banging closet doors as he searched for his rifle.

"My God . . . my God! Hurry, Sitko. Hurry! We've got to get the two of you outside! You've got to get him down to the guest house! Hurry! For God's sake, hurry!"

By the time I had pulled my brother halfway down the driveway, I could see Alexander standing at the door. A violent blast exploded in my ears.

"My God, you've killed them! You've killed them!" I could hear my mother screaming as I dragged Reno toward the guest house.

Grandma Amana rushed out of her room when she heard me shouting to her. Instantly she understood what was happening. An incredible power lighted her face as she placed her hands upon our bodies, making certain that we were not injured. Then she whirled about and ran into the pantry. In a moment she returned, her eyes wide, clutching a butcher knife.

"No one will harm you!" she muttered fiercely. "As long as I'm alive nobody is going to hurt you!"

Reno moaned in the cold night air. I took his face in both my hands and peered into his eyes. "Can you understand what I'm telling you, Reno?" I shouted. "Reno, we've got to get the hell out of here right now. Everything will be okay tomorrow, but right now we've got to get out of here!"

Without really understanding what was happening, he blinked at me and then turned, and with his arms wheeling he staggered after me down the road and out the front gate.

Fourteen

The rain pelted the windows. The sky seemed to reach down toward us with menacing fingers each time lightning flashed. The storm heaved against the steep streets of Silver Lake, pounding at our door. My brother was asleep, and I sat over a blank sheet of paper, unable to paint.

Now the wind raced around our tiny apartment, perched over the garage owned by one of Reno's friends who had offered us temporary shelter. The kettle hissed on the hot plate, and my brother murmured with distress in his sleep.

He was slipping away, day by day, into a place where I could no longer reach him. We had no money for a doctor. I was afraid of what was happening to Reno, but I didn't know what to do.

I tried not to think about it.

Reno groaned and I put another blanket over him. He had lost his job. Alexander saw to that. Reno had spent all his savings on liquor, and it took seven weeks to start collecting unemployment. Neither of us had any money, and we were running out of food.

I made tea and sat at the window, watching the sky go mad with grief. Finally I fell asleep.

Two weeks later, we got a message from our mother. I called her from a pay phone. She wanted to meet us at a coffee shop on Ventura Boulevard.

"Are you all right?" she asked helplessly.

"Sure . . . sure . . . I'm fine. But Reno should see a doctor or something. He's in bad shape."

"Both of you, meet me at the coffee shop and I'll give you a check," she said.

"Sure . . . sure, Mom."

Reno said he had a buzzer going off in his head. He said he had water dripping inside his head. I helped him into the bus while people stared at us. When we were finally seated, he smiled at me with childish affection, and I squeezed his hand.

Jemina was late, and when she finally arrived at the coffee shop, we had to wait for a table. Reno stared at her. When we were seated, he whispered into my ear, saying that he didn't trust the strange woman at our table.

I knew he was fading out. I knew he was vanishing into thin air, but I didn't know what to say to make Jemina realize how desperate the situation was.

"It was such a nice home for both of you," she whispered with tears in her eyes. "Such a wonderful opportunity for all of us. So you've both got to go to him and explain that you're good boys."

"It's no use," I said, twisting my napkin. "It's no use. . . ."

"I want you to talk to him," she whispered, her eyes darting frantically from side to side. "You just have to come home and make it up to him!"

"It's no good, Mom," I said. "It'll never happen. It's finished."

"No . . . no . . . don't say that, Sitko. Please don't say that. You never took the time to get to know Alexander. Believe me, he's a good man. He doesn't mean anybody any harm. He gave us a home and everything money could buy. He took us in when nobody would have us, Sitko. He's not a bad man, believe me. So you've got to call him, do you hear? And you've got to tell him how sorry you are," she begged in a pathetic little voice. "For my sake, Sitko, for me, you have to do this for me. You've got to make him listen so you can both come home."

I glanced at my brother. He looked as if he were slipping into the water and drowning. He shook his head and gasped for breath. The saliva began to flood from his mouth. He twisted in his chair, opening his mouth and gasping upward toward the ceiling. Then suddenly he began to scream. I lunged to restrain him as he tried to leap from his chair. All the people around us pulled away, whispering. Reno fell down. I could not hold him. He fell down, and when he struck the floor something inside him seemed to burst, and his body convulsed.

Jemina gasped and fell to her knees over him. I tried to help him to his feet, but his eyes had gone blank and blood began to run from his nostrils.

"My God!" Jemina was shouting. "Somebody help me! I think my son is dying! My God . . . my son is dying!"

At the hospital, my brother continued to shout and weep. They gave him a shot, and he faded away, lying on the sheets like a dead man. For days he remained unconscious. And then they took him away and strapped him down and shot electricity through his brain. Now he was quiet. He lay perfectly still in his white room, a vacant expression upon his face.

I stayed with him all day, returning to our Silver Lake apartment when it was dark. I sat in the empty room while the teakettle whistled on and on. And then I went to bed without eating, sleeping fitfully until dawn, when I could return to the hospital.

One day a man appeared at my brother's bedside. It was Jamie Ghost Horse. Somehow Grandma Amana had told him that Reno was ill.

I hadn't seen my father for so many years that I couldn't be certain it was really he. I kept trying to envision the man I had seen weeping in the hallway of Star of Good Hope. I kept trying to understand how this meek little man could be the tall, strong man who had been my father.

He seemed shorter now. He was thinner. The muscles on the left side of his face had collapsed and his features ran together. In his eyes was a terrible weariness.

He spoke slowly, as if he were reciting from memory. He touched Reno and spoke to him, but my brother did not recognize him. He lay perfectly still with a childish smile on his lips, gazing beyond Jamie Ghost Horse.

Our father gave me twenty dollars. He said that he had found an apartment for us in Oxnard. He said it wasn't a very good place to live, but at least it would be somewhere for us to stay until we found jobs.

"The rent is paid for two months," he whispered, without looking me in the eyes.

I stared at him in silence, unable to say a word.

"You were too young," he said, as if he understood my confusion. "You cannot remember me. But your brother . . ." he said, looking down at Reno. "I wanted to talk to your brother."

He was silent for a moment, and then he said, "That is all I have to say. Here's the address of the apartment. The key's in the mailbox. Maybe it will help till you find work."

He nodded aimlessly, looking first at Reno and then at me. Then he turned and left.

I stared after him, unable to grasp that this man was my father. I felt anger and confusion and longing. How could I let him slip away without saying anything? . . . Let him slip out of my life without saying a single word to this man who was my real father? But I couldn't speak.

A few days later Reno was discharged from the hospital.

He looked at me in silence as we took the long bus ride to a dusty little street in Oxnard.

"You okay?" I asked him.

He smiled and nodded, without replying.

I helped him up the stairs, and searched for the key in the mailbox. Then I unlocked the door, and got my brother settled in a wooden chair, while I let down the wall bed so he could rest.

We stayed in the apartment all the time, except when I went out to buy a few groceries with the money Jamie Ghost Horse had given us.

When we ran out of money, I called Jemina.

"You know how Alexander feels," she whispered over the phone. "If he thinks I'm giving you anything, he'll make a lot of trouble."

I waited for her to continue speaking, but she paused as if she wanted to hang up.

"Can't either of you get a job?" she asked at last. "Can't Reno get a loan from one of his friends?"

I didn't answer. I waited for her to offer some help.

"Alexander watches every move I make," she said. "He warned me that he'd throw your grandmother out of her house if I had anything more to do with either of you," she wept.

"Well . . . we have to have something to live on for a while. I have a good chance of getting a job," I lied, "but I can't get started till the first of the month."

"All right . . . all right," she sighed. "I can give you some money, but God help us if Alexander finds out about it!"

"Where can I meet you?" I asked.

"I can't leave the house. Your grandmother has been sick ever since you left, and I can't leave until the doctor comes."

"Well, I can't come there."

Then there was no sound. I feared Jemina had hung up on me or that Alexander had disconnected her. But finally she said: "You'll just have to take a chance and come by here right now for the money. He's at the studio, and I'll watch for you so you won't have to come into the house. Just stand down by the gate, and I'll watch for you. But hurry up because he'll be coming home soon."

I went back to the apartment and checked to make certain that Reno was comfortable. Then I rushed off to the house of Alexander Miller.

I did not know that Jamie Ghost Horse had been watching our apartment. I didn't realize that my father wanted to be near us but was unable to face us. It was so hot and I was so concerned about getting to see Jemina that I didn't notice Jamie Ghost Horse trailing after me at a distance.

He followed me to the house of Alexander Miller. He waited on the street and then he crept up the drive and stood among the trees, watching as Jemina hurried out the kitchen door and pressed a wad of money into my hands.

"Don't make any noise," my mother whispered anxiously. "He's been home for half an hour. He's upstairs getting ready for us to leave any minute. The doctor's already been here. So, for God's sake, take the money and get away!"

No sooner had she spoken than I caught sight of Alexander coming into the kitchen behind her. Hoping that I hadn't been seen, I rushed away as I heard Jemina saying: "It's nothing . . . nothing at all. I just thought I heard the nurse at the door."

When I got back to the street, I noticed someone up near the house, standing among the bushes by the front door. I was thinking that it was probably the gardener, as I reached into my pocket for busfare. Then for some reason I didn't get on the bus. The door hissed closed as I peered back at the house. At that moment, Alexander and Jemina were coming out of the front door. It was not until my mother had gotten into the car that I realized that the figure hiding in the trees was Jamie Ghost Horse.

Alexander Miller saw him at the same moment. He ran at him, yelling a warning to Jemina. But Jamie leaped into the driveway in front of the car and stood there without moving. Once again Alexander shouted as I started running up the driveway. Suddenly two shots burst in my ears. Alexander Miller stumbled and fell down. Birds burst into flight, rising like a black cloud over the trees.

I stopped abruptly and stared up the drive at the motionless body on the gravel. I froze as I watched Jamie Ghost Horse slowly circling the body of Alexander Miller and walking deliberately toward the automobile where my mother sat without moving or making a sound.

I shouted for him to stop, but nothing came out of my mouth. I watched as Jamie opened the car door. Then I winced and felt sick as my father fired two shots into my mother's body.

I remember the sound. I remember hearing the burst of the gun as I fell to my knees in the driveway, waving my arms in the air and yelling for help as my father ran past me and disappeared into the street below.

When I came out of Jemina's hospital room, there were reporters in the hallway. They gazed with an unspeakable fascination at the blood that had poured down my shirt and pants when I had carried my mother out of the car and into the ambulance. Their flashbulbs began to explode. They asked me about the rips in my jacket, where Jemina's fingers had clutched at me as she screamed in pain. They offered me money to tell them exactly how the shooting had happened. They stood in my path and would not let me pass, until, at last, an orderly shouted at them and pulled me into a linen closet where I leaned senselessly against the wall and panted for breath.

Finally it was quiet.

I sat on the bench in the hospital hallway all night. At six o'clock in the morning, they came out of my mother's room, wheeling her toward the elevator and up to the operating room.

"Is she going to be all right?" I murmured.

The nurse gave me a dark look, and I felt my insides dissolve.

"Of course . . . of course, she's going to be fine," a doctor chanted with too much reassurance.

When the elevator door closed, I wandered down the hall until I found the room where Alexander Miller lay in a coma.

The nurse said, "No visitors."

"I'm Seymour Miller," I said. "I'm his . . . I'm his son," I said.

She pointed to the door without speaking and waited for me to leave. Then she said, "Absolutely no visitors."

I sat back down on the bench in the hallway. I was worried about Reno. But I had to stay at the hospital until I found out about my mother. And so I waited. A constant procession of maimed and broken bodies passed by me, hour after hour. Women in wheelchairs. Men on crutches. Bodies on tables, wrapped in sheets. I could smell the pain. I could see it on the stunned and delirious faces of people who limped down the hall, their fragile bodies desperately scattered. The smell of pain was unbearable. I tried to think of Mrs. Blake and Susan Summer. I tried to remember the afternoon when we celebrated the completion of the magazine we had made. I remembered my grandmother and the marvelous courage in her eyes as she stood with a butcher knife, ready to defend us against all the demons of the world.

And then the doctor came to me and told me that my mother was dead.

The police drove me back to the house of Alexander Miller.

"He's not supposed to set foot in this house!" the nurse barked.

I hurried past the nurse and ran into the bathroom, where I became sick to my stomach.

Then as I came to my senses I heard a faint chanting coming from somewhere. I went in search of the familiar voice. In a tiny room behind the kitchen I found a withered old woman sitting in a rocking chair, her gray hair tied back and her long cotton nightgown so full that she looked like an overstuffed pillow.

As I approached, she smiled faintly and said: "We must imagine ourselves happy."

Then the old woman in the rocking chair looked up at me, and she trembled with fear, stammering: "*Kai-yo* . . . who are you? Who are you?"

"Grandmother," I whispered, "I need your help."

"*Kai-yo? Kai-yo? Kai-yo?*" she repeated again and again in fear, wincing as she pulled away from me.

Then she was silent. She rocked to and fro, and her arms hung between her legs. She would not even look up at me.

"*A-so-kin-a-ke* . . . Doctor," she chanted. "*I-yim-na-ke* . . . Police. *A-kis-sto-ma-too-ma-kon* . . . Automobile. *E-spoom-mo-kin-on*. . . . Help us!"

I embraced her, but still she would not look at me. Something had died in Grandma Amana. There had been something marvelous within her, but I could no longer see it. She had closed off the passageway to her heart, and I realized that she had left me somewhere far behind her.

And so I took her frail body in my arms, and despite the objections of the nurse, I slowly carried her out the door, taking her back to the guest house, where I put her to bed.

By summer Alexander Miller had come home to his big house on the hill. He dozed in his wheelchair and he ate his meals alone in silence. There were no more arguments.

Eventually he asked me to come see him, so he could talk about my grandmother.

"I gave Amana the house, and I'm not going to go back on my word to your mother . . . may she rest in peace," he said without looking at me. "And let's just forget about the rest of it. I don't blame you," he said. "You're too young to know what was happening. But your brother . . . that's another matter."

I agreed to stay with my grandmother and look after her, but only on the condition that Reno could live with us at the guest house. Alexander started to object, but I knew he didn't want any responsibility for my grandmother, so I insisted. Finally he agreed.

"You're my legal son and my heir, and I don't want people to say that I abandoned you after the death of your mother."

I smiled bitterly and shook his hand in agreement.

From that day, no one ever spoke about the shooting, but now Alexander Miller carried a large black pistol with him wherever he went. When he came to dinner, he would take the gun out of his belt and lay it next to his plate. And when he went to bed, he placed it under his pillow. He carried that revolver like a cane. It was his only companion for many months.

Then as he regained the use of his legs and began to go to the studio a few days each week, guests began to come to the house of Alexander Miller. And one day he told me that he was going to marry a woman I had never seen before. And she came to live with him in the big empty house.

Once a month I was required to have dinner with Alexander and his wife. We ate in silence. I glanced at this soft, submissive woman who now sat beside him, and I thought about my mother, whom he had never married despite her loyalty to him for so many years.

Alexander Miller had rarely worked at the studio since the shooting. His luck had run out, and he had not made a film in over a year. Eventually he began to accept bit parts in westerns and gangster films. Now he would come home at night with his orange makeup still on his face, and he flopped down into his big chair in a gloom. He panted when he climbed the stairs and he groaned when he sat down. The bullet wounds in his belly had left him ruptured and partially crippled.

I did not say good-bye to him when I left for San Francisco, where I had received a scholarship at the Art Institute.

Reno promised to look after our grandmother until the summer, when I would return home. He tried to be cheerful, but I could tell that he was deeply saddened by my departure, for we had come to love each other.

I went into Grandma Amana's room to say good-bye. She nodded incessantly and moved her mouth, but she did not speak. I put one of my drawings on her bureau, and then I stood looking at her. I was not certain that she even knew I was there. Yet I wanted to see just one sign of life from her before I left.

"O-ke. . . . Greetings," I whispered. The old woman lay like a velvet glove upon her rumpled bed, her long gray hair spread out upon the pillow. Her mouth was open and a trace of saliva still glistened upon her lips. "Grandma," I murmured, "it's me . . . *au-wah-tsahps* . . . the screwball."

She did not respond.

Then I walked to the window where the rain was splashing against the oak tree. I gazed into the clouds for a long time, and then very slowly I opened the window.

At first I could just faintly hear the splashing of the rain, but as I opened the window the sound grew. And when I had let in the wind and the splatter of drops flew into the tiny room, Grandma Amana gradually lifted her head and with a trace of light in her ancient eyes she smiled gently and murmured, *"SoodaWa!"*

Rain.

Fifteen

━ ■ ━ ■ ━ ■ ━ ■ ━ ■ ━

Now nothing remains but a cascade of fantastic images that pour from the fingers of Sitko Ghost Horse. The past begs to be remembered in his strong colors. He is the keeper of the hours and the days. They cry out from his paintings. The people and the names continue to live in his pictures. They are alive in his fingers as the darkness begins to come down.

The great house of Alexander Milas-Miller stands against the evening sky. The day is ending in a perpetual flood of moths. Nothing moves over the grass or around the tennis courts. The trees are fixed for a moment against the diminishing sky. And the wind stops to catch its breath.

The windows of this great house are closed and dark now. No one can enter or leave. Now there are no lights, no radios, no angry voices. Everyone has left this solemn house to face the night alone.

The paint on the shutters is beginning to crack and splinter. The lock that holds the front door closed aches with rust and the stiffness of old age. There are no butterflies in the *old oak tree, and birds no longer visit this forlorn house of Alexander Milas-Miller.*

The blue and white morning glories have begun their retreat. They will not bloom again. The grass has turned gray. And the night collects itself into deep shadows among the bushes where the footprints of Jamie Ghost Horse have filled with rain, though they can never entirely disappear from memory.

Weeds begin to grow in the graveled driveway where Alexander Milas-Miller's blood left its blemish. Jamie Ghost Horse laughs in a distant town and shouts to the bartender for another drink. The narrow door that flies open to the dead is always ajar in Gallup, New Mexico. Somehow that old man who was the father of Sitko and Reno vanishes into his own massive death. What remains is the everlasting screech of brakes.

Jamie Ghost Horse walks out of the bar and staggers into his one-eyed pickup truck. Somewhere on the old road between Gallup and Albuquerque he drifts aimlessly into the wrong lane, gazing into the wondrous illumination that is coming toward him. There is a great explosion. And then silence. Now he is fast asleep within his tomb of twisted metal and broken glass, beyond the reach of the policemen who hunted him for years.

And so the night hovers over the house of Alexander Milas-Miller, who puts aside his revolver and sits silently with his wife in the dark dining room.

"Jamie Ghost Horse is dead," he says. And his wife nods her head without speaking.

Occasionally a little man leads a prospective buyer across the lawn, but they never return. People are as alien to this old house as love and happiness. Beneath the oak tree a stone still marks the place where Jamie Ghost Horse threw the gun as he escaped into the street below. And sometimes when it is very quiet, passersby can hear the curious chanting of a crazy old Indian woman who still lives in the room behind the kitchen. But no one listens to her song.

Reno Ghost Horse smiles his bizarre smile when he enlists in the Marines, lying about his illness. After boot camp, he dies in the crash of a transport plane one day after leaving training.

Nothing remains now but this long, retreating day. Weary of the world, the house of Alexander Milas-Miller has closed its windows and drawn its blinds. The walls stoop with fatigue. The stairway creaks, though feet rarely ascend to the second floor where bedrooms are kept immaculately prepared for guests who do not arrive.

Alexander Milas-Miller comes home with orange makeup still on his tired face, and he groans with pain as he flops into his big chair. He stares into space and mumbles nothing in particular. Sometimes he sleeps, but he never goes upstairs to bed anymore.

His wife sits beside him and watches silently. From the little room behind the kitchen comes the chanting of Grandma Amana as she makes imaginary beadwork and chatters in a garbled language to Sitko's pictures on the walls.

No one turns on the lights. No one disturbs the sheet-covered furniture in the living room or leaves footprints upon the polished floors. No one calls. No one knocks. No one shouts or speaks. There is no laughter. And nothing ever happens here. Until one hot Sunday afternoon, when Alexander Milas-Miller slowly hunches over a glass of water and swallows a fistful of pills. When it is almost dark they find him bobbing lifelessly back and forth in his chair, his arms thrown back, his robe open to reveal the deep blue scars upon his belly, and urine slowly trickling down his white, hairless legs.

Grandma Amana shouts and falls to the floor, a bit of imaginary beadwork still clutched in her brown, wrinkled hand. The doctor is summoned, and she is put to bed.

Night is coming. Grandma Amana tries to fill her lungs and mumbles the names of long-forgotten friends. Far Away Son . . . SoodaWa . . . Weasel Woman . . . Amalia. You can hear the names all around, humming in the oak tree as Grandma Amana calls out to them. She cries for her dead daughter and for the grandson killed in a distant land. And then she smiles peacefully as she dreams of Sitko who sits by her bed day and night, working feverishly to paint all the memories that pour from her. "I will keep you alive in my visions and my pictures," Sitko pledges as Grandma Amana spins the marvelous tapestry of her life in the night air.

A spider creeps undisturbed across the windowpane. But nothing else moves. Nothing happens. Nothing begins or ends.

Yet in a brittle soil in some distant time and place, under fragrant eucalyptus trees where children still sometimes play, a herd of brilliant sweet peas rises high above the ground. No water flows to nourish them. No hands extract the weeds that strangle them. Yet miraculously they have survived, making their way through the hard, ungiving land and climbing high into the air. Now in this longest night their blossoms pour a heavy honey into the air.

In her bed Grandma Amana is awakened by the fragrance of the flowers. Slowly she reaches out to touch the Fox that waits beside her bed, and then the beadwork tumbles from her hand.